We Met In The Fog Book One

# Cole

# Magnus

Grace Edgewood

Edited by Allie Heady

Author photo: Olivia Merritt

Interior design by Allie Heady

Cover design by Allie Heady

For Abby-

Thank you for always being my first

and most important reader

"No one ever told me that grief felt so like fear"

--C.S. Lewis--

# Table of Contents

# Chapter One:

## New Town, New Me

There was no way this was safe.

Jumping from a train was dangerous, especially when chased by angry ticket examiners. I urged her to run faster as we darted around disgruntled passengers. I jumped over the handbag of a wealthy woman and smiled as I grabbed the bag's handles.

"Harold!" the woman howled, "He stole my purse!" The man with her did not seem that worried. He looked as if he wished I had snatched her instead. I dug through the bag as we ran and took out a velvet coin purse. I pushed the coin purse into my pocket and threw the bag behind me without looking back. I felt no small amount of joy when I heard the man chasing me grunt on impact.

She had reached the end of the car and I watched as she struggled with the door handle. I tried to slow down. I barely avoided slamming into her and instead let my shoulder grind me to a halt on the cold steel of the door. I wrestled with the handle until it swung free. Several of the passengers screamed as the door pulled inward and wind whipped in around us. She jumped over the gap that revealed the ground rushing beneath us and kept running. I turned to catch a glimpse of our pursuers over my shoulder. They were gaining ground. I jumped after her and I balanced carefully on the metal pin that joined the train cars together. I stretched backward and slammed the door shut in the man's face.

I scurried inside the next car and fastened the door shut behind me. "Sorry, excuse me!" she yelled as we barreled into a dining car. People gasped and moved to either side.

"Outta the way!" I yelled as I ducked under a waiter's tray. People jumped out of the aisle and dove into seats.

In the last car, we found only an elderly woman napping in a seat. I jumped over her bag and kept running.

At the end of the car, we watched the tracks fly under us. I ran to the left side of the train and gripped the rail into my ribs. I leaned out and threw my head into the wind. The air was bitterly cold. If I swung out far enough, I could see the name of the railway company painted in sun-faded red on the side. I squinted through the wind and towards the town in the distance. The sign bearing the town's name was growing rapidly. A valley filled with rustling maiden's grass swept down beside us.

"Stop!" someone yelled from behind me.

A quick glance over my shoulder confirmed that the

ticket examiner and two men in black clothes were closing in behind us. I left her peering over the railing and ran back to the door. The men vaulted over the old lady's bags just as I bolted the door shut. I could feel the heat of the car leaking out under the door. The icy metal bit at my exposed toes. I joined her again by the rail. She turned to me, fear prominent in her eyes. The wind whipped her hair over her head. Her hand immediately moved to rest on mine. Her fingertips were cold against my hand. Her face begged me to come up with a plan.

It was beginning to spit snow. If we wanted to get away undetected, tracks in the snow were not helpful.

"We'll jump!" I yelled over the roar of the wind.

She nodded and gripped the rail with white knuckles. I maneuvered her to the side of the train that did not have sharp sticks and boulders waiting to crush us. In other words, the side with the softest looking grass.

"The train is slowing down!" she yelled.

The wind took her words and flung them away from us. Pointlessly I yelled back, "Stopping soon!" I looked for an opening in the awaiting valley. They would catch us for sure if we waited for the train to come to a complete stop. I looked back over the rail and towards the town. I could almost make out the town's name now.

Banging and shouting ensued behind us. The guards had finally caught up. The screech of a train whistle and the hiss of brakes cut through the air.

"Get ready to jump!"

She grabbed my hand, fear plain on her face.

I could finally hear above the roar of the wind. "Don't worry," I shouted as we ducked under the chain that guarded the exit. "It'll be fun!"

I gave her hand a squeeze. The guards were still trying to wrestle the door open. We had to hurry. We stood with our backs to the rail and watched our window of time closing.

"3," I counted down.

"2," she continued.

"1!" Then we jumped. We tumbled violently down the grassy hill beside the train tracks. I rolled head over heels until I skidded to a painful stop at the bottom of the dell where our bodies were hidden among the high reeds of grass. Our quick descent had beheaded several of the fluffy, white stalks and I knew I was covered in the fine hairs that were now dusting the entire valley. We came to rest in the shadow of the sign I'd seen from the train. I raised my head to read what it said. Welcome to Carlin! It practically shouted at me with its curvy font and aggressive red and gold color scheme.

I remained flat on my back with one leg drawn up and I stared up at the blue sky, and I tried to catch my breath, but was startled when the reeds behind me rustled. I craned my neck just as her eager face popped out from the weeds. I smiled in recognition as all fear vanished from our faces.

For the first time in a long time, Lyla laughed. "Let's do that again!" she gasped. Lyla picked blades of grass out of her hair and threw them into the wind. She stretched in the tall grasses that surrounded us.

I smiled and sat up slowly. We'd made it. We hadn't jumped too late and hit the sign; we hadn't jumped too early and caught the tree. I grinned wider as I heard a train whistle announce its arrival at the station in Carlin.

I laid back down in the dirt and grass to rub my tired joints. They begged for a break from the lifting, running, climbing, jumping, and all the other strainful things catching the train had required. Lyla, however, was ready for the next adventure.

As she danced around me excitedly, the sun caught her bronze hair and reflected back streams of red gold. If our faces weren't enough to give away our blood relation, her hair matched mine and our mothers. Unlike me, her eyes belonged to only our father. She had his soft gaze that mimicked a crisp winter's sky, while I had eyes the color of autumn leaves. According to Lyla, I had gold flecks in my eyes, which "reflected my inner worth," or so she says. I think she reads too much poetry.

I watched her slender fingers brush the tips of the tall grass and caress the tender snowflakes. Those hands crafted her own dolls and clothes, but her smile never wavered.

I looked down at my own hands. I saw bloodied

knuckles and a crooked finger. Memories of the guard I had punched to avoid getting caught on the train and other desperate things I had done surfaced, but I pushed them away. Focusing on the past wouldn't help me survive right now. I suppressed a groan as I hefted myself off the ground.

Now that I was on my own two feet, Lyla ran toward me. "Tell me again!" she said eagerly.

I rolled my eyes. "I've told you a thousand times!"

Her eyes pleaded with me to continue.

I sighed, and the puff of my breath was visible. "We're going to Rolling Acres. There, the only thing in the country is mountains. Right now, I bet those peaks are just bursting with color. There will be valleys full of nothing but wildflowers. You could roam for miles and not find another person. We'll make ourselves a little house and plant some food. Then, when the winter comes, we'll sit out on our back porch and watch the snow fall slowly down from the mountains. There won't be anyone to chase us or hunt us down. We'll be free."

Lyla smiled and looked towards the little town that was our last stop before crossing the border. She grabbed my hand and gave me an encouraging squeeze. It wasn't much of a walk to the first cluster of buildings. The farther we ventured into town, the longer the walk would be getting back to the train, and we had to sneak on for just one more trip. Rolling Acres was just on the other side of the Calfkiller River.

While we were still in Leangap, I overheard a traveler talk of the vast mountains there. He made it sound like a man could live there for a song. I had been pick-pocketing the man at the time. After his revelation, I withdrew his wallet and scurried off to tell Lyla of the plan forming in my brain. We could be free if we could only make it to Rolling Acres. Its vast terrain and difficult navigation would make it impossible for local law enforcement to find us. It held the promise of freedom, the plea of normalcy to return.

We blended into the crowd but always kept our hands clasped to each other. Judging from the dirty streets and lack of political banners and slogans, it was safe to say that we were at least a day's walk from the nearest big city.

The town had once been a bright and colorful seaside village. The fabric awnings had been complementing shades of gold and crimson. Today, only the sun-bleached remnants clung to the skeletal remains of buildings. The storefronts were tattered and begged for dusting. Snow had gathered on the windowsills and on the roofs of the houses in the distance.

A carriage rolled past us. Judging from the fair-skinned inhabitants and green attire, they were executives from Leangap. Leangap was a several-hour train ride to the West, usually far enough to keep Leangap authority at bay.

I'd visited Leangap several times. All for mostly illegal reasons. The Duke who lived there had a price on my head that would turn even a noble's head. I had stolen from him and humiliated his family in the process. I think his daughter enjoyed the excitement, but Castle Farfalle's walls seemed to shrink quickly. His guards were ruthless and eager to serve his unpaid judgment. They hadn't been kind, and I still bore scars from that misadventure. I never made the mistake of getting caught again. His gallows waited for the day my neck would rest in his noose.

He wouldn't have pursued me this far. Would he? That was months ago. He could have quickly replenished his storehouses and stables by now. My eyes tricked me into seeing threats in the sun-filled stalls and mercenaries in the shadows.

Amid my reminiscing, I had squeezed Lyla's hand painfully tight. "Cole," she said, shaking me out of a daze. "Someone is following us."

I let go of her hand to cautiously look around. When she thought I was not looking, she rubbed her fingers.

"Look at those beautiful melons!" I exclaimed. She took the hint and wandered to the stall selling fruits. She stayed near the back of the crowd, so I could see her no matter where I was in Towns Square.

I walked to a tall storefront with my hands in my pocket, trying not to look suspicious. I glanced around the open courtyard. No one seemed to take any particular interest in me. I meandered to the darkened space between two buildings. Standing silently, straining my ears to hear if someone was approaching. When no one followed me into the shadows, I began looking for a different plan. I looked up at the tall brick building as a small smile spread across my face. It was time to test my climbing skills. I slid my fingers into the gaps in the stone and smiled a little more as I slid my toes into the small spaces between the cemented stones.

It was moments like this that made my attire so fitting. My shirt was too big, so it was tucked into my pants that were also a size off. Cords were tied around my shins and down to my ankles to keep the ragged edges down. It made jumping from moving trains, scaling rickety buildings, and dodging unseen attackers much easier when I wasn't tripping on my own clothes.

I gripped the brick and began to climb. Once I reached the thatched roof, I paused, letting the winter breeze brush over me. I grabbed the edge and pulled myself over with the skill of a dead fish. I moved from beam to beam, trying not to fall through the dried grass. Stepping carefully to the edge, I crouched down to avoid being seen and scanned the area. I grabbed the edge of the roof and tried to keep my footing on the unsteady straw.

Lyla stood innocently at the fruit stall, smelling an apple. A hundred people bustled around on the harsh winter's day. The smell that rose from the market was repulsive enough to make me gag. The scents of sweat and animal droppings mixed with the raw meat being sold. I scanned the throngs of people, looking for danger. A butcher was taking out his frustration on a slab of meat. There was the baker's son who was lugging sacks of flour. There were very few children running about. Families gathered and gossiped.

Prominent men dressed in black stood by the pub,

but they did not seem to be immediate threats. They appeared to be doing the same thing I was. One of them jumped a little, then shoved another one as I watched. He pointed to the fruit market, then they all moved as one. They began shoving and elbowing people aside and making their way forward. Startled, I looked at Lyla; she searched the ground for me. Should I wave and get her attention, or would I also attract unwanted attention? The men were headed toward her, but they didn't see me. I needed to keep it that way. I leaned out over the roof to find the fastest route to her. I saw the fabric awning lazily swaying in the wind a fair way down from where I squatted and decided to take my chances. I took a steadying breath and jumped.

My stomach rose into my throat as I fell. The fabric was weather-worn and thin, so it barely gave any resistance. I hit feet first and rolled to even out the point of impact. I hit the stones hard, but Lyla was at the forefront of my mind, not my injuries. A pile of snow slid off the roof and down my back.

I saw the men only because of how uniquely tall they were. I knew there was no way I could fight them. They were tall, muscular, and obviously trained. On the other hand, I was scrawny, average height, and my only experience came from a life on the run. I had made my living through deceit and tricks. This would be no different. A plan came to me as I bolted up. The fabric awning had been shredded as I fell through it, but one large piece remained pinned under me. I grabbed the thin cloth wrapped it around my hand.

I got up, and I rubbed my shins. The men in black had reached the storefront. My feet slapped the dirt and ice-crusted cobblestones as I ran down the street. I didn't see Lyla, but she was clever. She had hidden somewhere. The only problem was that I was not with her and she had hidden

so well, I couldn't find her. The men were pushing their way

through the multitudes. I ran as fast as I could to the crowd. I

dodged around people and around children who stood

gawking at the action. I pushed past as many people as I

could until I reached the line of men sweeping the crowds.

The men left a large wake for me to follow, but I could not

move past them. With my heart nearly beating from my chest,

I unwrapped the fabric from my hand. The cold air stung my

fingers as I draped the fabric over my head holding the ends

of the snow-dampened cloth tightly under my chin, I hunched

over and diverted into the crowd. Unsuspecting pockets and

purses volunteered valuables as I meandered past the rich

folk. I borrowed a worn traveling cloak from a stranger. He

yelled and chased after me, but he was old and too frail to put

up a fight. I was young and ready for an adventure. I got a

bowl from another store and put my newfound riches in it.

"Give your spare change?" I pleaded, coating my voice in lies, "Money for the poor and needy."

I stumbled and fell in front of the men. I landed directly onto one of their feet. I made a show of standing up and brushing it off. "Please forgive me, sir." I bumbled and stumbled around, causing as big a scene as possible. I finally tripped and spilled all of my coins.

"Get out of my way!" he barked.

"Beggin' your pardon, sir, but who are you lookin' for?"

"A little girl and a boy menace, know them?"

I bobbed my cloaked head enthusiastically. "Yessir, yessir, I does. She ran thataway!" I pointed back towards the train.

"Sir, isn't the train scheduled to make a stop soon?"

I heard the man's breathing accelerate. He ran towards the train faster than I thought possible for a man that size. I bent down to collect coins and watched them run away. They were all dressed similarly. Each wore loose pants for running, a tight-fitting shirt for climbing, and shoes that fit snuggly. Their hats veiled their eyes in shadow. I continued with my charade of picking up coins and stumbling around. Coins were scattered all across the hard-packed dirt and stone. Puddles claimed a few, and I wasn't eager to stick my hand into the frigid, discolored water. A small, soft hand touched mine when I reached for a coin.

"Thankin' you kindly, ma'am."

"The least I can do for the man who saved my life more times than I can count."

I winked at her.

"Meet me behind the bakery when you can," I

whispered.

She nodded and handed me the bowl. I slipped a couple of coins in her hand as she scurried away. I took it and headed east, while she walked west, towards the smells of baking bread.

I returned most of the money I'd taken, then ticked through the list of things we needed. I felt the bag I'd taken from the rich woman in the train thump against my leg. Its weight gave me small reassurance that we weren't out of moves just yet. I found an empty burlap sack the apples had come in and walked around the square. I couldn't find the old man I'd taken the cloak from, so I just took off the hood and left the front clasped around me.

I tried to spread out the money best I could. I was a talented thief. I didn't like stealing from people who were struggling to survive like me. Maybe this new town was a chance to turn over a new leaf. Find a job, set down some roots. It was a nice thought. As I snuck through back alleys and around shady businesses, I knew I was set in my ways. Perhaps Rolling Acres would be different. If I could just get across the river and to the mountains, everything would change for us.

She was waiting for me amid the heat of ovens and the heavenly smells of dough. She slowly emerged from the shadows. She held out bread that was a few days old and the rest of the coins. As nervous as the previous encounter made me, I was grateful to be in her presence again.

I ran to her. "Are you okay?" I asked frantically.

"I'm fine," she said, laughing. She stopped abruptly and said scornfully, "Cole, you're bleeding!" She pointed to my skinned elbows.

"I'm fine, but I think we should probably get out of

here."

"Agreed," I looked around for the men in black or another issue. "Where?"

I ran through a list I had been making in my mind as I poked around town. I looked down at my pocket. Any good thief would tell you that I had money in that pocket, but it wasn't nearly as much as I had started out with. The bag of coins that I had tied at my waist was now small enough to fit in my pocket. Our buffer was shrinking significantly." There's an inn south of here. I'd love to stay there, but those men were looking specifically for a little girl and..."

Lyla's wide eyes told me she wasn't listening. "Men are coming over here, and they're glaring at you," she whispered.

"Ignore them, let's walk the other way," I said calmly, but inwardly my heart was pounding. We walked swiftly back towards the market. Sometimes I wanted nothing more than to be out of the public eye, far away from open places. Maybe that's what made Rolling Acres so appealing. But there were other times, like now, it was helpful to have so many people around. Two children could easily get lost in a crowd this size.

We did our best to avoid the hulking figures that dwelled in the shadows. I counted eight in view, but more lurked in the shadows like beady-eyed scavengers. I had tucked the scrap of fabric I used as a disguise into my apple sack. My fingers twitched uneasily, wanting to be helpful. I wanted to rip out the fabric and cover Lyla's head so badly. I vainly wished to grab her hand and run, but I knew that would draw attention to us. And what we needed most of all was to be ordinary.

My heart skipped a beat. I saw two buildings so

close together they were practically one. We slipped between them and to freedom. There was a rickety wooden fence behind the buildings that we scaled without any problem.

From there were tiny houses and rolling hills. It was all very quaint and simple looking. Rather appealing given the life I lead. I kept glancing behind us, expecting some evil entity to appear. After several false alarms, I decided no one was following us. We passed an old farmhouse with a whistling tea kettle howling from inside. There was a worn fence that took us around to the barn. I saw the hen house from a distance and took the chance. We jumped the fence and ran to the tiny structure in the fading light. I hoped no one was at the rear window to see our desperate escape attempt. We came upon an old hen house the owner wasn't using. The hay was dry and clean enough to use.

I laid the cloth down for Lyla to sleep on. She

smiled when I curled up next to her.

"No guard tonight?"

"We're in an abandoned chicken coop, about half an hour's walk from town. I'd say we are safe enough."

A branch snapped somewhere nearby. Lyla tried to hide her laugh when I stiffened. Out of instinct, I hopped up to peer around. I couldn't see anyone other than an old woman coming out the back door to stand at the back porch. She stood there for a moment, gazing into the night. I held my breath until another voice called out from the flickering halo coming from the door. "What's the matter, Cecile?"

"Thought I saw something," she hollered back to her husband. She meandered back to her rocking chair and sat down. An elderly man with a short beard came to sit beside her. He puffed on a pipe, and she leaned her head back. Other than the occasional creak of her chair, they made no other noise. Cows munched nearby, and the old silo groaned in the wind. The snowflakes were growing in size, so the snow would be stopping soon. The magnificent white contrasted greatly to the stark of the night.

I sat back down, and Lyla gave me a hint of a smile. "Safe, huh?" She gently hit my arm. "Relax."

She laid back down and waited for me to follow. I swiveled my head one last time, then laid beside her. It was frigid. She shivered against the bite of the wind and snuggled closer to me. I draped the stolen cloak over us and wrapped my arms around her, she nestled her head on my chest. I could hear her every breath. I knew she was counting the beats of my heart.

"Cole?" She shifted to look up at me.

I blinked hard. Watching the snow dance outside had nearly lulled me to sleep. "Yes?"

Lyla readjusted on my chest, hugging her cold fingers to her chest. "Why were those men after us?"

I paused. I had an idea, but I didn't want to scare her. "I don't know," I said. Some Lord or Duke had probably gotten tired of my shenanigans and sent his men out to find me. Once I was caught, we would be imprisoned. If he was feeling particularly ill, I might be whipped and beaten. I probably would be anyway.

She sat up and looked around. She looked down at me, worry plain in her eyes. "But they won't catch us, right?" she asked, panic seeping into her tone.

I blinked hard, trying not to fall asleep. "Of course not." I shifted, so our eyes were mere inches from each other. "I would never let that happen."

She laid back down and snuggled closer to me. "What's our next step from here?" She whispered.

A smile brought on by nostalgia crossed my face. This was a game we used to play as kids. When life got too hard to bear, we would simplify it to one choice at a time. One baby step that turned into a hundred. Eventually, the combined effort would get us to the logical end. It was easier to not get burdened with life when your outlook told you the giant steps were really just several small ones.

I tucked one arm behind her and the other behind my own head. "We'll go back into Carlin, and catch the train. Then we'll be home free." She sighed happily and snuggled closer. While getting comfortable, she poked me with her icy toes. My leg recoiled from the unwanted cold. "Gosh, Lyla! Warm up your feet a little!"

She laughed. "Goodnight." I felt her long sigh of breath warmth onto my chest. "I love you," she whispered as if we were children again.

I smiled even though she couldn't see me. "I love you, Lyla. Sleep well."

Her breathing grew deeper. I was left alone, staring up at the darkened roof of the chicken coop. All I could do was lie in silence and listen to the sound of the wind.

# Chapter Two:

# Back-Alley Charades

The following day, we decided to risk the town once more. This brought the worry of capture and the promise of something new. A new pair of clothes, a new shop to steal from, a new town to be banished from.

I had realized long ago that my mind had two modes: prank mode and Lyla mode. Sometimes it was hard to keep both sides from merging into one chaotic mood. If I didn't shut off the side of me that was always on the run and fighting to stay alive, I found myself not being the brother I'd promised to be. Other times, while scurrying from place to place, my Lyla side got too headstrong. I gave out trust or the benefit of the doubt to every stranger we met. That always ended in my arrest.

Then there were other times, like now, when both sides of my personality worked together simultaneously.

I snuck up the worn wooden steps of the farmer's house. I climbed the front porch's beam and climbed inside through an open window on the second story. I touched down quietly in a meek little bedroom. The floorboards squeaked underneath my silently stealthy feet. I would have nicked a piece of jewelry had any been available. I snuck into the closet and picked out a nice-looking dress, a pair of pants, and a shirt.

Feeling strangely alone, I crept down the stairs. No one was home. The kitchen was empty except for a singular pot left over the coals of the stove. Keeping the Sunday lunch warm, I guessed. Hopefully, the church service would last long enough to return the clothes I needed.

A traditional dress for Lyla, and actual pants for me.

I left her in the henhouse while I changed outside. I sat down to untie the cords I had around the base of my current pants. The edges were ragged and worn, but the rope kept them tight to my legs.

The new pants were crisp and unknown to me. It was strange, feeling the extra material brush by my ankles. I still didn't have any shoes, but I didn't want any. The wind nipped at my toes, but I had never liked having shoes pinch at my heels. The shirt was still too big. I tucked in the tails and walked over to a water trough. I certainly looked different. I ran my fingers through my hair to calm the beast.

I heard Lyla giggle behind me. I turned around. She smiled and twirled the edges of her skirt. Her tall, weather-worn leather boots peeked out from underneath the frill. Her smile granted me a glimpse into her joy in this small moment. I smiled back at her and extended my hand. "My lady," I said, bowing. I slipped into a fake accent. "Don't you look ravishing this evening!"

She did the same. She rolled her eyes and took my hand, "You're too kind, my lord."

My smile fell slightly; she really did look fantastic. This is the life she should have had. She should have been in school and complained about her teacher. Casual dresses like these shouldn't awe her.

I wished vainly I could give her everything she's missed out on. I wished she had a best friend she could giggle with. I wished she had a house to go home to, and parents who supported her. I would give anything to see her happily installed in that life. I would hand it over without batting an eye.

But my hopes didn't change anything. I twirled Lyla around and watched her gleefully smile.

"Alrighty, ma'am, let's get moving."

She smiled and started running back to town. I smiled and chased after her as well. She may not have had an ordinary childhood, but we had each other at least. I had her to be my whole world, and she had me for protection.

I sincerely enjoyed running through the open fields barefoot. I loved feeling the soil squish under my feet, and the grass brushing my ankles. I especially loved watching her pause to pick the buttercups that poked their shy heads out of the snow. She stopped to twirl amid the tall corn stalks.

We reached town sweaty and panting. We did our best to blend in with the other children gallivanting about while the church bells released the sermon.

I had a little money left in my pocket, so we began gathering things we might need before moving on. Another cloak, a used pack, another flask for water, and some matches. Finally, we started rummaging through the trash outside the seamstress's shop. I could easily slip inside and steal a needle if needed, but we were looking for extra material.

The word tasted sour in my mouth. *Extra.* We'd never had anything extra. We barely broke even most of the time. Everyone here seemed to have no problem throwing out the too-small shoes or the yard of fabric that no one had used. Didn't they realize people needed their spare?

Lyla emerged from a bin smiling. She brandished a length of blue material just long enough for a patch or two. She ran up to me, rubbing her fingers over it appreciatively.

"Isn't it pretty?" she asked.

I smiled. The fabric had little doves soaring across the length of it and the blue matched Lyla's eyes. Something crunched at the head of the alley. I sidestepped in front of

Lyla to get a different angle and I ducked as quickly as I could. I pushed Lyla towards the brick wall, pressing her against the bins in the hope of keeping her out of sight.

"Stay safe," I mouthed. Lyla nodded. I would have loved to remain hidden with her, but I knew the men in black had already seen me.

I stood again, pretending to have dropped something. As I rose, I tucked the invisible something into my pant's pocket. I took a few steps forward, keeping the space between the two bins covered. I had a degrading question on my lips, but I barely got turned around. They were on me faster than I could blink. Someone hit the back of my knees hard. I tasted the dirt of the alley. I rolled over as quickly as I could to get a swing at whoever hit me.

He punched me repeatedly before throwing me back against the ground. He ripped the cloak from my throat, leaving me gasping in the dirt. I tasted blood. My right ear rang painfully loud, and I blinked stars from my eyes.

I seemed to be moving in slow motion. I grabbed the bin to help me stand, and turned to throw a punch; instead, I froze. He had Lyla pinned beneath him. One fist held her throat, the other enormously huge hand held both of her fists. His knee kept her legs pinned down so she could not kick him. All fight drained from me. I lowered my fists slowly. "Please," I begged. "Please, leave her be."

The man grinned. He began squeezing. Lyla tried to scream, but he cut her off. She squirmed under him. She tried to fight back, but he didn't act like it made a difference.

"No!" I yelled, jumping forward. "No, take me, leave her!" I pushed at him, clawed at his face. Shoved him with all my body weight. I punched him anywhere I could reach, but nothing fazed him.

"Please! I'll do anything you want! I have a little money, you can have all of it. I'll admit to any crime across any kingdom. I'll arrest myself, but please, save the innocent."

The man snorted. "Innocent? I've been told you're a fate worse than death."

"She hasn't done anything wrong!" Her lips were blue, and her face was pale. "Somebody help us!" I screamed, but his other three accomplices guarded the mouth of the alleyway. As if anyone was decent enough to help a street rat like me. I continued clawing and pushing the man. I did everything I could, but he was nearly triple my size.

A shadow passed over me. I was afraid to look. Perhaps it was another thug coming to remove me from the situation. Maybe a hugely irrelevant bird had passed overhead. Out of the corner of my eye, I saw a person in a billowing traveling cloak. He stared intently at Lyla's assailant.

My mouth went dry. Were the gang and this strange man a team? I couldn't fight off one man, let alone two. The cloak hid any identifying characteristics, but he seemed much smaller than the thug. The man began mumbling something in a rhythm under his breath. The trampled weeds beneath the thug's feet began to multiply. I took a step back, wary of whatever magic possessed them. Somehow, they evaded Lyla. She didn't get a single scratch from the thorns creeping up the man's legs.

The man called out in pain and let go of Lyla. I pulled her up and held her tightly. Her eyes rolled back in her head as she coughed and gagged in my arms. She turned her face toward the wall of the alley. I pressed myself against the bins, as far as I could get from the tangle of vines but I kept my eyes glued on the fight in front of me. The thug tried to pull the vines off of himself, but the more he pulled, the faster they grew. The cloaked man whirled towards the thugs guarding the entrance. He scooped up some dust from the ground and blew it in their direction. It whipped around them, blinding them. Without warning, the very ground beneath them opened and swallowed them whole.

A strangled gasp escaped me. I scooped up Lyla and ran out of the alleyway. I barreled past the cloaked man and into the land of the living. He silently watched me go. I saw his hand flick towards the thug. The vines tightened quickly, and a sickening snap echoed down the alley. "Cole," she wheezed.

"Don't worry," I said between breaths as my feet pounded into the square. "We're getting out of here."

I turned down another broad street, hoping the

bustling of people would camouflage our escape. I stole a glance behind me; there were more men in black following us. Before I could turn back around, I ran into someone.

I started to apologize, but it was another thug. I turned to run, but he was quicker than I was.

He ripped Lyla from my grip. "No!" I yelled. He shook her, causing her hair to fly violently as her head whipped against his strength. "Stop it!" I screamed. I punched and hit the man repeatedly and clawed at him, trying to get Lyla back. I didn't see the man I was hitting. All I could see was Lyla.

Someone hit me over the back of the head. For an instant, I lost control of my body. I fell into the dirt like a lifeless sack of potatoes. I blinked hard, trying to clear the stars from my eyes. My head throbbed and I tried to gain enough sense to stand. "Cole!" Lyla screamed. She doubled her efforts to escape.

"Quit thrashing!" the thug told her. This man wasn't as strong as the last one. Lyla kicked and squirmed and finally began getting loose. As he tried to grab her again, she pushed away, hitting the brick wall of the alleyway. There was a sickening thud, and Lyla was still.

"Lyla!" I screamed. I took a deep breath, feeling the rage fill me. I felt dizzy from standing so quickly, but I had to get Lyla out of here. Something in me snapped. A strength I'd never felt surged through me. I tore into the man who'd thrown her, punching and pounding until he was a bleeding mess. All the men were facing me, snarling and popping their knuckles. I picked up a broken piece of glass in one hand and a sharp stick in the other. The men readied their knives, fists, and all the other weapons I clearly didn't have.

I took a deep breath and charged, howling my battle

cry. The men ran at me silently, as they had obviously been trained. Before I touched any of them, a commanding voice boomed from the entrance to the alleyway.

"Stop!" The voice ordered. We all froze. Even though I knew I shouldn't have, I turned to see who could command such a presence that even the mercenaries obeyed.

It was the man who had stopped the thugs in the seamstress's alleyway. Why were there so many people fighting over us?

A wood plank struck the back of my head, then I got a boot to the back of my knee. My eyes rolled back in my head as I hit the ground. I fought to keep my eyes open, but my head pounded me into a haze. I coughed up a splatter of blood onto the dirt then blinked hard, trying to get my bearings again. I clawed my way toward Lyla, afraid to touch her. What if I hurt her more? My fingers brushed her shirt. I fingered her hair for a moment before brushing it away from her face. I saw a shiver of movement. Her eyes fluttered, and her face contorted in pain.

I looked away from Lyla and saw the hooded man leap past us, cloak billowing in an impossibly strong wind. He summoned fire from the apartment kitchen nearby and covered a man. Water came from deep in the ground and smothered another man. A gust of wind threw two men over the building. Finally, the last man was swallowed by the very earth he stood on. It all happened so fast. All the while, I clung to Lyla, trying to shield her from the battle before us. Her eyelids fluttered, but she still did not move. How could I have let this happen? We were so close to Rolling Acres, to freedom. How could we ever live out that dream now? I could never make it on my own. The lights around me seemed to dim, living seemed less sweet. If she died, then I might as well go with her. I tried to keep the tears from my eyes. The fight wasn't over yet.

When the man finished with the thugs, he sensed my gaze. He stood again and let his arms hang freely by his side. He addressed me but still did not turn around "Yes, young man? You wish to speak?"

I fumbled for words. What did I say to the man who just saved our lives? "I had that," I complained selfishly. "I could have taken… seven fully trained men in a dark alley. Before you and your…." I moved my hands as the man had while causing the strange events. "...before you won the fight." His silence was more frighting than the fight was. The only move he made was to glance at me over his shoulder. Taunting a hooded magician wasn't the noblest way to die. I wished I had just kept my mouth shut. His steady gaze drifted from me to Lyla. I followed suit. In desperation,

I gripped her arms and shook her gently. "Lyla," I whispered

hopelessly. "You're going to be okay," I mouthed, unable to

find my voice. "I'm sorry."

"Here, let me," the man said tenderly, fully turning

from the opening on the alley.

I clung to Lyla's body and scooped her into my lap.

The man lowered his hood and knelt beside me. "Just let me

help." His face relayed a kindness that his previous actions

did not portray.

In the books I'd gotten Lyla, wizards were always

old and decrepit looking men who could bust out moves

faster than I could. This man fit none of those descriptions.

His chestnut beard was well tended to and closely cropped.

He had deep-set eyes and a warm flush to his cheeks. The

corners of his eyes held laughter wrinkles. His fingertips were

cut and calloused from the thousands of pages he had turned.

I saw something there that made my fingers loosen their hold. I knew, had the roles been reversed, and it was me in Lyla's arms, she wouldn't hesitate. I knew Lyla would like the strange man. But I also knew I had no other choice. What else could I do to help her? I was useless in this situation.

I nodded at him. He smiled kindly, then scooped up a little bit of the dirt beside me and found some dirt from his pocket. He mixed them together then blew it around us. The world melted into nothing but brown and dark. I squeezed my eyes shut and kept my hand firmly in Lyla's. We weren't trapped in the whirling storm for long, but it was long enough for every fiber of my being to convince me I had made a colossal mistake. This was the consequence of letting the part of me that trusted too much take the lead.

I'm not sure how, but when I opened my eyes again, I was sitting in the shadow of a large cottage. The rough-hewn stones that made up the outer walls told stories of long nights and hard rains. The roof looked sturdy and well-attended to. Spring had come early here. Around me, blooms of all colors imaginable filled the air with the smell of Eden. Small windows with crossing grids were swung wide to allow the prowling breeze inside. The heavy wooden door was rounded on top and wide open. I noticed a small garden to the side with leafy herbs fighting for room. Tomatoes, carrots, and cucumbers all looked ready for eating. A heavy-laden blueberry bush hunkered near the front door.

I patted myself down, praying I was still alive. I squeezed Lyla's hand. Her face grimaced. Without warning, a warm yet gentle breeze lifted Lyla's body evenly. She floated there as if waiting for me to rise too. I struggled to stand. When I did, my head spun. I held my head in my hands and prayed it wouldn't explode. When I managed to step forward, the breeze hoisted her to be even with my shoulder, then tenderly brought her inside. We passed through a bright kitchen and into a spare bedroom. She was laid gently on one of the two beds waiting there. I knelt down, unsure of what to do so I gripped her hand and prayed for a miracle. I rubbed my eyes and let my head droop a little.

"I had hoped you'd find me on your own," said a voice from the doorway.

I whirled around, and there stood the man who'd saved us in the alleyway.

A million questions ran through my mind. Every emotion wanted to register on my face. I fought to quiet the storm and wrestle the waves into submission. "Where are we?" I finally croaked out.

He unclipped his cloak and hung it over his arm. Finally, he looked at me. A warm smile spread across his face.

"Welcome to River Haven."

# Chapter Three:

## River Haven

He turned to hang his cloak on a hook on the wall beside the door. I craned my neck, trying to see him from around the corner. "Who did you say you were?"

He walked back wearing earthy tones that reminded me of the warm sun and rich soil. I watched him in fascination as he floated Lyla aside.

"I didn't." He gave me a small smile. "But you may call me Saxe. Mark Saxe."

I was still wary of him. I got up to watch him as he got his supplies, then found myself following him into the cottage. He did not speak to me as he got ingredients and strange tools from the kitchen. He approached in the bedroom doorway and knelt beside Lyla. I grabbed his arm before he touched her. "So, you're a wizard?"

"Of sorts," he replied as he gently pulled his arm free. He moved two of his fingers in a circular motion, and Lyla rolled onto her stomach.

I got between him and her unmoving body. "What are you going to do?" I demanded.

He shook his head. "She's in good hands, Cole." He looked up at me, expecting me to move. "You look hungry. Help yourself to anything in the cottage."

With one flick of his hand, the winds that had brought Lyla here pushed me out. I dug my heels into the wood grain of the floor, but I barely slowed down. "Wait, no!" Once out of the door, I turned quickly, wanting to protest. He smiled and shook his head. I began to protest again, "She's my sister, I need to-" the door snapped shut. I leaned my head against the door and groaned. I put my fist against the door with the intent of banging on it or barging in. Instead, it thumped softly against the door and stayed there. He had closed it with such authority I didn't dare try to open it again.

I slid down the door and sat there. I paused, not wanting to leave Lyla and longing to learn more about this unassuming house. I stood silently, afraid to let him know I wasn't right outside. My curiosity brought me through the hall and into an open kitchen with many windows. It was tidy, in a chaotic, lived-in sort of way. The cabinets were made of living trees and their bark formed the handles and hinges. Small pieces of moss blanketed parts of the cabinets in the soft carpet. The kitchen island was made of intertwined roots supporting a smooth rock with rounded corners. It looked like an enlarged river rock. There was a large cabinet that intrigued me the most. When I put my hand on the handle, I could feel no heat emanating from it. It was strangely frigid.

Several cold gusts of wind circulated the box when I opened it, keeping the contents cold. "Incredible," I breathed. I stuck my hand inside the box. The wind stole the heat from my sweaty palm. I laughed under my breath in amazement. I shut the door again and ambled around the kitchen. I opened cabinets, pulled on drawers, looked under shelves, and perused their contents.

After finding nothing interesting, I climbed down from looking in the tall cabinets above the cold box. I jumped down and walked closer to the kitchen's island. The smooth stone had a woven wooden bowl in the middle of it. Apples, grapes, and oranges overflowed the bowl, so I grabbed an apple and rolled it absentmindedly from hand to hand.

As I stood there, the roots shaped a stool for me to sit on. The vines grew to form a back on the stool, complete with the letter "C". I could only assume it was for Cole. I wondered if Lyla's chair would have an "L ." It was the right height, width, and size for me to sit comfortably. When I finally sat down, it pushed me close enough to rest my scabbed elbows on the stone. I bit into the apple, expecting the dull mush that usually came from the fruit I stole from markets. Instead, a crisp and tart taste filled my mouth. I took another bite, then another, thoroughly enjoying myself.

A flit of movement caught my eye. I hopped down and watched as the stool dissolved back into the living vines. I walked back towards the bedroom but took a right where a large sunroom awaited me. There was a large carpet in the middle with a small table. Comfy-looking chairs were scattered about, all facing the vast windows. I peered out and saw luscious green hills blanketed in soft sunlight.

A raven sat on the window sill and cocked its head

at me. When I walked into the room, it fluttered its wings as if to get my attention. I walked closer to study it. I put my hand on the glass, amazed at the clarity. The raven gave me one long, annoyed caw, then flew swiftly away.

A shiver slid down my spine. I longed to feel the sun on my own back. The glass that had been captivating a moment ago now seemed more like prison walls. I hurried around the corner and into the kitchen then strolled out the front door and into the meadow. Across the yard, I saw a widespread yet shallow stream with tiny waterfalls. Beside it was the tree the apple had come from.

I smiled. Here, in the sunlight, my worries seemed to melt away. I walked over to the river bed and stepped into the cold water. Small rocks scattered underneath my feet. Grass sprung up near the edge of the river. Hidden frogs sang from the reeds, and birds built nests from the grasses. Small minnow darted about playfully. Across the river, a mountain jutted from the water. I peered upstream and saw more water and more mountains. This must be a river that fed into a giant lake.

My heart skipped a beat. Could this be the Calf Killer? Could we really have traveled that far in such a short amount of time? Lyla and I voyaged for weeks, and now we're only a swim away from Rolling Acres. A thought struck me like lightning. What if this was the Rolling Acres side of the river? We could already be there!

I climbed the tree's branches to look from a high perspective. I couldn't see the lake, only the promise that it was there. I could follow the current around the bend until it dumped into the Narrows if the current was correct. The Narrows is the thin stretch of ocean that spreads along the shores of Leangap and up to Rolling Acres. The port at Carlin was the only way to get across them. Usually, the only passengers were from Leangap. It was faster to go by land, but bandits roamed freely between Mine Lick and Eagle Creek. The locals called the impassable territory the Savage Gulf. The port also took boats to and from the old island in the middle of the Narrows, but it was abandoned centuries ago. No one came in or out. It was said a strange creature guarded its shores and slaughtered anyone who dared set foot in the water. I'd never believed the old wives' tales, but people still whispered about it.

I climbed down into the spotty shade until I found a curved branch perfect for sitting. I lounged there in the shadow of the magnificent tree, swinging my legs lazily and watching the sun dance on the water, I thought of my days as a younger boy.

I had never known my parents, not well anyway. I

had a few scattered memories, but all I had to remember them by was Lyla. I loved Lyla more than I could ever love myself. I knew the deeds I had committed to keep us alive, but she didn't have to. Thinking of her brought on a wave of emotions I'd kept hidden. My heart ached for her lost childhood, for her unusual upbringing, for the parents she would never remember. And most of all, for her current state. What if those men had hurt her badly? What if she died?

What would I do then?

A bird hit a sharp note above me. I stiffened and looked around. The open-air of the meadow was no longer appealing. The noise of the water's rushing turned sinister. I longed for more than sunlight and apples for company. I jumped down and hurried back into the house. I moved through the hall, past the kitchen, and to her door. Not a sound escaped the room. Something kept me from banging on the door, from barging in and demanding news. Why had I ever left her? Why did I keep letting this one side of me rage out of control? When would I learn to stop trusting people?

Nobody would help us.

Nobody wanted us.

No one could be trusted.

I slid down with my back to the door and wiped the apple juice off my hands and onto my pants. I glanced back down before realizing that these weren't my pants. These were the farmer's pants. I'd never gotten the chance to take them back.

I looked to my left and saw a bare wooden staircase leading to an upper level. With one last look at the door, I couldn't make myself open it, so I stood up. I wanted to get a full scope of the cottage. I investigated every window, door, corner, every possible hiding place. I started up the staircase, but the second stair squeaked. I stopped, expecting the man to come barreling out of the room. Saxe, I think, was his name. I continued up the stairs. At the top, there was a landing. The door directly in front of me was closed and probably locked. The entrance to my left was cracked. What luck for me.

I slipped inside.

On my left, there was a fireplace with embers still glowing. There was a large desk and so many books I couldn't read all the spines. A threadbare rug sat on the floor between the desk and the fireplace. Directly to my right were shelves full of strange specimen jars.

Creatures I'd never seen and never thought to imagine floated or swam in jellies and waters of all colors. Fireflies that lit up in electric blues, purples, and oranges floated lazily in a jar. Eyes that followed me around the room sat next to it. A tiny person with wings sat in a small tank on the bottom shelf. She had a little house made of sticks and leaves, a well, and lots of sand. She flew to the glass and pounded on it when I got closer.

I jumped back and walked towards the desk, trying to convince myself that I hadn't just jumped out of my skin for a pixie. There were papers scattered around the desk. All the papers were in the same handwriting, but all kinds of languages. A cup of pencils and paintbrushes sat in one corner. A small cup of water dyed with paint sat next to a scrap of paper. His watercolors sat drying on a corner of the desk. I picked up the piece. It was a sketch of myself, this exact moment. I wore the farmer's clothes in the picture, leaned more on one leg than the other, and held a scrap of paper. My heart pounded, and I stuffed it in my pocket. My eyes darted around furtively, looking for him to appear magically as he had in the alley. Nothing happened. I took a deep breath and leaned on the stool, trying to calm my racing heart.

Something thumped against the floor. I whirled around, half expecting the pixie to be acting up again. No one was there. A notebook was sprawled on the floor. I could only assume I'd bumped it. I picked it up carefully, casting an ear to the door as I did. The hall was silent as ever. I filtered through the pages and saw that they all had the same title.

I set the notebook on the table again and took a closer look at the papers on the desk. I opened the first paper. There were four symbols with words scrawled beside them. On top of the form were three words in all caps.

THE FORESEEN FOUR.

My brow wrinkled while I tried to comprehend the notes. On the next page was a description that barely made sense. It sounded like the description of a dream.

I ran my fingers over the words, trying to read them. Rather than understanding, a void of blackness washed over me. I felt myself fall for an instant and I struggled to catch myself. I rolled down a hill and came to rest in the shadow of a mountain. I gathered myself slowly, trying to comprehend what had happened to me.

I rubbed the back of my head and turned to look at the hill. I saw three silhouettes standing together. In front of them, a fourth slowly walked up the slope. The three each hit the silhouette with whatever kind of magic they could. I couldn't see what the magic was. All I saw was a burst of light and the fourth person stumbling. But the silhouette never stopped. One by one, they fell. Until only one was left. The two fallen comrades melted into the shadows as the real showdown began. They faced each other as the wind and the rain raged out of control. The two were mere inches from each other.

I felt the impact before I saw it. I fell backward onto the rug. I got up as quickly as I could. How much time had passed? I stuffed the papers in my pocket for further inspection and ran down the stairs. I sat down in front of the door and took a deep breath. What had just happened? My mind raced, and my fingers searched for something to fiddle with. Then I remembered the contents of my pocket. I felt for it and it was still there. It lay crooked besides the watercolor I had stolen from upstairs.

I pulled it out to inspect it in the magical light filtering through the auburn-stained windows. I had stolen a compass from inside Mark Saxe's pockets as he had passed me. He'd been so busy with Lyla, he hadn't noticed one of my hands slipping into his coat. I had been hoping for gold coins or a knife; instead, I got one worthless item barely worth the time it took to nick it.

I thought back to the strange dream I'd experienced upstairs. It felt so real. Who were those people? Why were they fighting? Who was going to be the lone victor?

The door I was leaning on suddenly swung out from behind me, and I fell backward.

Saxe looked down at me. "You didn't go far," he commented, looking down on me.

Startled, I sat up quickly. I tried to lean around him and see into the room. The door snapped shut before I could glimpse Lyla. My face flushed. "Says the man who loves home so much he carries dirt with him." I got up and brushed myself off. "Seriously," I looked up at him again, "get a hobby."

He chuckled. "Come, there is much to discuss." He stepped around me. He turned sharply and ascended the stairs.

With one last look at the door, I stood as well. Nervously, I followed him up the stairs to the study.

I admired the room as if in a new light. When the wizard had entered, the room came alive. Tiny lights I had failed to notice began to come up. The pixie seemed a little less angry. A spark ignited in the fireplace and slow flicker began to consume the wood in the hearth.

There were two comfy-looking chairs on a rug in front of the fireplace. As Saxe drifted over to the desk, the end table between them shifted to the right of one chair. The two chairs turned to face each other.

He leafed through the papers on the desk. "You came up here." It wasn't a question.

"You said the whole cottage," I explained nervously. "So I took that literally."

He took a deep, steadying breath. I tensed, bracing

for the worst. "Cole," he paused. And in that instance, I died a million deaths. What if something had happened to her while I was off exploring? What if he had hurt her and I wasn't there to stop him? Why had I been so trusting? He interrupted my series of thoughts.

"She'll be fine."

I sighed heavily and heaved myself into the nearest chair. With one weight off my chest, my whirlwind of questions came to the surface. I tried to let all of those negative thoughts I was harboring leave, but there was one question I couldn't let myself drop. Why had I trusted this man to begin with? "So, what are you exactly?" I asked slowly. I didn't trust myself to let the questions spill out. I needed to find a speck of immoral dirt on him. "Not a doctor, by the looks of it. You definitely have some unique interests."

"The show in the alley was impressive, if I do say so. Quite taxing, though," Saxe sat just as heavily as I had.

"I was talking about the dirt again, but..." I trailed off when he shot me a look. I cleared my throat, "Right, so you're a wizard of some kind?"

"You could say that."

"You *have* said that, but what do you call it?"

"Studying. I've studied the elements and my books of spells enough to memorize incantations, movements, and thoughts." He gestured to the shelves around us.

Each odd piece around me would seem out of place in any other library. But here, they each were a piece of a master puzzle. The catty-cornered seat, old whiskey barrel, and the random artifacts gave the room its style. But I didn't see any kind of tools that could have lifesaving qualities. No bottles labeled "elixir of life" were within reach.

"How does that help my sister?" I asked. I was always hesitant to accept help. I am always prepared to be independent and never be indebted to anyone.

"I can perform feats that any man would call miracles. I can change the forms of matter and bend the fabrics of space and time at will. A broken spine shouldn't be too much of a stretch."

There was a map on the wall near the window. But it wasn't covered in unique places and magical-sounding words. How did Saxe know how to do this? How did I know for certain he was telling me the truth? I wanted to pick his brain before letting myself trust him. "Where did you learn all of this? Were you born into this profession, or is there a magical school you had to go to?"

Saxe gave me a small smile. "Magic tends to run in families, but with enough practice, anyone may learn."

I felt a little cheated. He hadn't really answered my question. How did I know for sure Lyla was okay? I began to be wary of the silence from downstairs. "Did you just study 'magic' or do you study a part of it? How do you know how to reform skin and bone? I don't know if you noticed, but she isn't a planet or the flow of time."

"You seem to have taken a sudden interest in magic, Cole."

I shrunk back a little. "No. Magic is just something you don't hear a lot about in my line of work."

"Which is?" he said.

"Brothering," I replied.

A shadow passed over his usually composed expression. "I see."

I leaned forward. "Speaking of which, how can you be certain my sister is alright?" I insisted.

"Well, Cole, I'm not a doctor, I'm not skilled in medicines or lifesaving miracles-"

"Are you trying to make me feel better or worse?" I was beginning to feel nervous. Was he going to ask for retribution? What would he do to us if he is as skilled as he claims? Should we just run while we have the chance? Rolling Acres was so close, I could practically taste freedom in the breeze.

"But," he continued. He held up his hands for a dramatic effect. "I have something else. Magic. She'll make a full recovery."

"But how can you be sure?" I heard the desperation I was fighting so hard to cover up.

He looked at me in a different light. "You're just going to have to trust me."

I lowered my head in shame. He probably was a

good man. Most likely, he deserved a little trust. After all, he had saved Lyla when I was unable.

"I was hoping to gain an apprentice while she's here." He had a mischievous twinkle in his eyes.

On second thought, perhaps I was wrong. Saxe was a scheming wizard with an alternate agenda and a troubling plan. I knew the doubt was evident in my eyes.

"She's a young girl," he coaxed. "Don't you think a little magic will brighten her days?"

I sat forward on the very edge of my seat. Assuming I was faster than his magic, I could quickly get around him or overpower him. "I've got enough to keep her entertained." I was ready to escape at the slightest sign of aggression.

"I understand you're a pretty talented thief." He gave me a knowing look. The paper, picture, and compass became heavier in my pocket. "Your self-defense could use some improvements. A little magic might help."

I weighed the expenses of the idea. A safe haven for Lyla to recover in. A talented wizard watching over us. Free food, shelter, and new trade to learn.

But what were the drawbacks? I certainly didn't know the consequences of meddling in magic. What if he kept us trapped here? Were we just an experiment to him?

Then I looked into the eyes of the man who had offered. There was honesty and deep devotion, not only to his craft but to me. I'd never seen that level of love in anyone in a long time. "Fine," I can't believe the words had left me. "But only a few lessons."

"Excellent."

He began to stand up, but my questions weren't answered.

"So, are you a mind reader?"

He looked at me queerly and sat back down slowly. His expression made me wish I hadn't asked. He looked down at me like I had caught him picking his nose or using the restroom in my rose garden. He was hiding something.

"You know my name, Lyla's name. And you know I stole something from you."

"Reading someone's mind is an invasive and dirty business," he said evasively.

I paused, expecting a fuller answer. "And?" I crossed my arms. I wasn't getting up until my suspicions were proved true or otherwise.

"People have private thoughts for a reason. If they wanted to share, they would speak up. Thoughts belong to that person alone; it is no one else's business perusing your memory files."

Good answer. I still couldn't shake the feeling that

there was something odd about Saxe. What if he was lying?

"But could someone have that ability?"

"You ask good questions, Cole," he commented gratefully.

"And I'm usually denied answers," I answered.

"Yes, it is possible. However, under my guidance, you will learn no such thing."

"Sir, you didn't answer my question. Are you a mind reader?" He opened his bearded mouth to answer, but finally, an idea struck me. I jumped up. "Wait! I'll take a man's actions above his words any day. Let's test you." I walked to the fireplace and secretly withdrew the compass. "Now! What do I have in my hand?"

He rolled his eyes. "My stolen property."

"Which is…?"

"My compass," he flicked his fingers, and the

compass zoomed out of my hands and into his. "Sit down, Cole."

"No, that proved nothing. You could be knee-deep in that dirty business you're talking about. Turn around." I pretended to look over his mantle for something to select, but really I only plucked the papers from my pocket. "Now, guess!"

"The clock?"

"That thing looks like it weighs more than I do! You threw that guess away; give a real guess."

"The magnetic rock," he said finally.

"Is that what that is?" I smiled. "You can turn back around." I handed him the stack of papers and sat down again.

The old wizard's eyes widened.

"Never grab a thief's shoulder," I explained. "The

hand it's attached to can do anything. Besides, I thought the compass was real gold."

"Did you read them?" he said, panicked.

"I never said 'read'," I explained, thinking of the strange vision I'd gotten while trying to read them. "Is there any... magic on those?"

"No," he studied me carefully, "just ink. So you don't know what's on them?" his panicked tone prompted me to lie.

"I just read the title. Who's the Foreseen Four?"

He sighed, obviously relieved I had no knowledge of what the papers contained. "Just an old prophecy. Nothing to concern yourself with."

Coming from anyone else, I would have gladly believed him. I would have strolled out the door after helping myself to his pockets once again. I might have taken Lyla and made a mad dash for Rolling Acres. I would have freely

forgotten about this whole encounter. But there was

something in the way he looked at me that made me question

his statement. His eyes matched the bright fields outside, but

their soul contained a sadness that seemed directed at me. His

lingering stare made me believe that there was much more on

those papers than what I knew.

He tore his eyes away from me and faced the

window. "Do you know why those men were after you

today?" His tone was casual, but his eyes were worried.

I racked my brain. Had I angered any foreign

delegates lately? Probably. Did I owe money to a high and

mighty King somewhere? Definitely, I had completely lost

track of who hated who and why they hated me. "I probably

stole something from their employer, don't know why they

would waste time and energy to track me down, though."

"Who was their employer?"

I shrugged. It could be anyone. A wealthy senator, a sultan, or even a network of gangs. "I steal from a lot of people."

"So you have no idea why they would be after you?"

"Maybe it's for my devilish good looks," I smiled at him and winked.

He rolled his eyes and stood up. Things began putting themselves back to how they were before our little chat. His chair turned, and the end table slid between us. My chair began to turn with me still in it. I found myself facing the dying coals. Books laid out on his desk came flying at me to sink back into the crowded shelves in front of me. Papers shuffled themselves together. Paintbrushes, pens, and pencils began to put themselves away. I could only watch in amazement as the room tidied up.

He smiled at my small-minded wonder. "I think you and Lyla will be safe here, at least until you are ready to face the world again."

I whipped around in my chair to face him. "What's that supposed to mean?"

# Chapter Four:

# Nothing to Lose

He eyed me carefully. "Cole, look at those walking sticks. Pick one out and follow me." With that, he swept dramatically out the door and down the stairs.

Nervously alone and entirely confused, I browsed the broad selection of walking sticks that sat in an old whiskey barrel. Why would I need one of these? Most were covered in a thin layer of dust and didn't look like they had seen much use. Many had enjoyable qualities, but some had strange markings. I looked at one that was smooth and curved. When I tried to pick it up, it slipped in my hand. I left it alone, knowing that I would need a firm grip if we went hiking. The second had too much bark, so it flaked off in my hands and was top-heavy. The third wasn't smoothed at all, so it gave me splinters. Finally, I saw one near the back of the stack. It had a curving design carved into it with a light hand. The top was forked, but the rest was straight enough to lean on. It felt right in my hand, so I grabbed it and ran down the stairs.

I had only been alone for a few minutes, but I was already tired of it. I feared silence would await me. The silence that would welcome unneeded thoughts and the fear of the worst. I would hear the voices that echoed my self-doubt and the bone-shaking fear of losing Lyla. I didn't trust myself to brave that silence.

I thundered down the stairs, testing each stair for a squeak as I went. Only the second from the bottom and forth from the top was of any danger. I rounded the corner and walked into the kitchen. Birds flew in and out of the open windows, and rainwater collected in a basin in the corner.

This room was indeed a marvel of modern science. On second thought, magic was the one to thank for this. The tree outside had been perfectly molded into the house's framework. Its leaves draped the window in the shade, so the sill was not in direct sunlight. That meant that the steaming pie that sat there now could cool adequately.

When I had walked through here earlier, there had been no food to be seen. Nothing on the stove, nothing in the brick oven, nothing on the counters. Now, the whole house was alive with the smell of baking bread and the sounds of sizzling meat.

I watched the old wizard in amazement. He moved about the kitchen with comfort and ease. He flicked a finger at a cabinet, and the twig-covered door swung wide. He turned his back to check the food as two plates waltzed off the shelf, drifting down slowly like it was all an intricate dance.

When I could tear my eyes away from the extraordinary display, I found Saxe bent down to peer inside a stone hole in the wall. He reached inside with a cloth wrapped around his hand and pulled a fresh loaf of steaming bread out of the burning pit. The smell alone was enough to make my mouth water. A seat formed beside me, emblazoned with "C" again. I sat eagerly.

He studied me carefully. "I see you've explored down here as well." He turned back to the oven. He grabbed a tube of olive oil and began to pour some into a shallow bowl.

"How could you tell?"

He began sprinkling spices on top. "The seat. No adjusting, no hesitation. Also, it formed with a 'C' already on the back."

He came forward with a plate of steaming meat pie. I noticed a chair formed for him as well. The back had a large, swooping "S."

A question popped into my mind, and slipped out before I could think twice. "Why is your letter bigger?"

"When you can reanimate that tree to keep your cottage alive while simultaneously managing to keep the house from falling in on itself every day for years, then you can have a larger letter. But for now: my magic, my conjurings, my house. My letter is bigger."

"Right…" I craned my neck to find Lyla. It was tranquil. He picked up his fork to eat, but I waited for Lyla to join us. "Where is Lyla?"

He dabbed his mouth with a napkin. "In your bedroom."

"My-" I stopped myself. That wasn't important right now. "Isn't Lyla joining us?"

His face saddened. He dropped his napkin back into

his lap and slowly laid down his utensils. His eyes diverted to the table. "Cole, I must confess that I lied a little bit earlier."

I froze, my water glass halfway to my mouth. "About what?" Humor had always struck me as an easy way to catch someone off guard. Another way to get in an early punch. It had become my armor and my first line of defense in this dark and dangerous world. I forced a grin. "Personally, I hope it was the whole 'needing an apprentice' thing." I opened my mouth to continue, but then I met his eyes. I knew instantly that he was referring to Lyla. "What's wrong with her?"

He rested his elbows on the table. "I'm afraid those thugs have done permanent damage. On her own, she would never walk again."

I slid off of the stool, feeling unsteady on my own two feet. A wave of dizzying anger swept over me. I pushed bak from the table. I kept my stance was wide, and my fists balled, ready for a fight. "You said-" He stood up suddenly, cutting me off. I took several steps back.

"I know what I said!" he yelled, trying to talk over me. He took a deep breath and put a hand on the table to lean on. "But I also said 'on her own'." His tone was much calmer now. He set the walking stick on the table. "Put your hand on it, Cole."

I hesitated and rubbed my fingers nervously over my palm. This man had just lied to me. What else could he do? Was he trying to suck my soul into the stick so he could live forever? That was a crazy idea, but it genuinely crossed my mind. I had no idea what he was capable of.

He gave me a knowing look and gestured for me to step forward. For the first time in my life, I did as I was told. The tree bent down to completely cover the window as he began mumbling. The candles snuffed out one by one. The smoke began to swirl around us. I wanted to let go, to run away, but he kept his hand firmly on top of mine. The smoke shot straight for the staff with a loud clap of thunder.

The tree snapped back into position, and sunlight flooded in. The candles flickered back to life. He lifted his hand, and I slid mine off absentmindedly. All I could do was stare at the magical artifact before me. Saxe smiled at me and handed me the staff. If I looked closely enough, I could see a faint hint of blue visible in the carving. It was as though the very core of the cane was the magic itself. It emanated from every crack and every etch.

As I ran my fingers over the now-glowing pattern, he sat down heavily. I stood beside my chair and memorized every inch of the walking stick. After a moment of silence, he leaned forward and said, "Just make sure Lyla has this. She will be fine."

"You keep saying that, yet you also just told me you lied to me."

He sighed and ripped off a piece of bread to dip in the olive oil mix.

It was a long and silent meal. The sun had set, and the moon was rising. The only thing on my mind was Lyla, and how good the pie was, but that was at the back of my mind. How would the staff help her? Granted, it was a magic staff, but magic couldn't fix everything.

Could it?

After my second piece of pie, I stood up slowly.

"I want to see her."

He finally looked up at me.

"Now," I protested. It probably wasn't wise to taunt a wizard. Why couldn't I just hold my tongue?

He swept his hand towards the bedroom door, and the latch clicked. It swung inward slightly. I hesitantly walked forward. I put my hand on the smooth wood of the door and pushed. "Lyla?" I croaked as the door swung in.

There she was. Right as rain. She was sitting up by leaning against the wall. She read a poetry book while simultaneously eating a slice of meat pie. Saxe had brought these to her, but I had no recollection of when.

"Cole!" she said happily.

"Hey," I offered quietly. The absolute stillness in her legs was impossible not to notice. I knelt down beside her bed. "Are you in any pain?"

She shook her head, a slight smile playing on her face. "You worry too much. I'm fine, really. He's a miracle worker."

I handed her the staff. "Let's pray for one more

miracle then."

The moment her fingers brushed it, life came back into her lower half. A foot restlessly twitched, a knee shifted into a more comfortable position. Her laugh cascaded over me. I knew she was going to be okay. Saxe had indeed worked a miracle.

"Thank you, sir," Lyla said, looking above me. I turned to see him standing silently in the doorway.

"Please, call me Saxe."

I met his eyes, "Thank you. Thank you so much."

He nodded and closed the door behind him. That's when I noticed the bed on the opposite wall. I got up and sat down on the soft cotton sheets and quilt as if in a daze. I looked around the room in total amazement before facing her once again.

It was a simple room with one window between our

beds. The floor was worn, and a faded rug lay on the floor between us. A nightstand was beside my bed, and another beside hers. A small bookshelf with only three shelves was under the window with a pitcher of cold water and two glasses on top. The stone walls cast shadows that the invading moonlight struggled to cut through. I looked up to see her sitting as I was. She faced me with a look of absolute wonder on her face. It was a marvel of magic and a home for the homeless.

I smiled at her. "Well, you won't have to worry about my cold toes poking you tonight."

She laughed again, but it wasn't as genuine. "It will be strange not having you for warmth."

"Hey, if you really need my cold toes that much, I'm only right over here."

She smiled at me. Her eyes drifted to the open

window between us. "It's beautiful here, Cole." Her eyes roamed the countryside. "He told me that you'd agreed to apprentice under him." Her eyes found mine. Her hair, unruly and frizzy due to the day's events, shone brightly in the moonlight playing across her face. "Why? It's so unlike you."

"Well, on the one hand, it's magic. And we've got nothing to lose. Why shouldn't we jump at the chance?" I paused and leaned forward. I felt the walls had ears, and every breeze was a spy. My heart began to beat faster as the excitement and adventure of it all crept upon my senses. "I think that's what he wanted."

"What do you mean?"

"Something is going on here, Lyla. Can't you feel it? Magic flows like water through this house." I smiled in excitement, but she didn't share my sentiments. "He has secrets," I continued, "secrets men would kill for. Isn't it strange how he offers them freely to us? I intend to find out

what's really going on here. Before it's too late."

She was silent for a moment. Her face portrayed a

raging sea of emotions crashing and beating on her. I saw the

fear and worry mix with anger and excitement. "I think

you're right on all accounts but one." She finally looked up

from her hands. "I do have something to lose. *You*." Our eyes

met through the expanse of moonlight. "Be careful, Cole."

With that, she rolled over and became silent.

# Chapter Five:

# Practicing Patience

The next several days were the best I could remember. Every morning I awoke well after the sunrise, in no rush to forsake a safe nook or hitchhike to a new city. This was the longest stretch I had ever remained in one place. Each new day greeted me with singing bluebirds and never-ending spring. Saxe's cooking was the best I'd ever had. Every meal was offered freely and regularly. Like clockwork, each night we all sat in the sunroom to watch the sun go down. As the stars came out to play, Saxe would tell stories of the solar system and the magic of the worlds beyond ours. In turn, Lyla and I would tentatively tell stories we had heard from our years on the run. He was eager to hear how the outside world had progressed. It was a peaceful paradise I'd never known.

The only drawback to living here was that every morning started the same way. I woke up, stretched, and walked into the kitchen. Lyla would be sitting at the island, chatting with Saxe. Bleary-eyed and stiff, I would join them.

And every day, like clockwork, I would sit down next to Lyla. Her chair did, in fact, have a cursive swooping "L" on the back. Saxe would greet me with a smile and give me a steaming plate of food. And every day, without fail, he would ask me one question.

"Good morning, Cole. How about a magic lesson?"

And every day, the conversation ended the same: a stiff and resounding no. But today was different. When I offered my answer, he didn't accept it as final. Instead, he studied me carefully. "I think you would excel in elements. Why don't we start with those?"

I ignored the question and took a massive bite of eggs and toast. Saxe gave Lyla a knowing smile. I felt a sudden, unexplainable stab of betrayal. When did they become such good friends? Had they planned for this to happen? I thought Lyla was against me getting involved. I finished my country-fried ham and guzzled the rest of my water. He was calling my name excitedly.

"Was this plot concocted by you?" I asked as I placed my dishes in the sink.

"I'm sure I don't know what you mean," she said, innocently toying with her new walking stick.

"And what, pray tell, will you be doing while I suffer out there?"

"I'll become a martyr for the cause. While you keep him busy out there, I'll be doing some digging of my own up here." She pointed up the stairs. "He's all the time writing stuff down. His library's bound to be full of helpful stuff."

A smile cracked across my face. "Oh, I see, Miss Sneaky Minx. I'll ask some questions of my own."

"Give me a heads up somehow when he finally comes in."

"I'd forgotten how mischievously sneaky you could be."

She shrugged. "I learned from the best."

She gave me a grin before darting up the stairs and I was left with the fleeting impression that I had just started her career in thievery. I shook off the sly smile and marched myself out the front door.

He dragged me the rest of the way outside and told me to stand by the apple tree. I hadn't been given an option, but I didn't refuse. He had been the definition of hospitable, and we hadn't exactly been easy company. Especially when I considered that Lyla was now pillaging his personal files.

I gazed up at the window on the outward-facing wall of the office as Saxe droned on about magic's origin and other unimportant things. What was Lyla finding up there? Was the pixie bothering her as it did me? Were there really piles of answers gathering dust up there? Were there more secrets to uncover? More hidden backstory? More to this old man than meets the eye?

"Cole?" he nudged me, and I came barreling back into the real world. I stood on his meticulously overgrown lawn, in the shade of his towering apple tree.

He smiled warmly. "Observe, Cole. I don't want to have to stitch you back together."

That caught and kept my attention. I didn't want to end up in four separate pieces scattered around the valley. I would be of no use to Lyla then. As I watched, he bent down and dipped a finger in the stream. He rubbed the water onto his hands and began the magic process. He concentrated, then moved his right hand in an arc above his head. The water followed suit. It danced and sparkled in the high arch, bringing a few pebbles and fish with it. It playfully splashed back down when Saxe turned to me again. "Your turn," he announced.

"Er, a few questions. First: how? Second: why?"

He gave a weary smile. "Well, pick one, and I'll answer it first,"

I pointed skeptically to the stream. "Why do I need my hands wet?"

"It's just a habit, but it does help kick start your magic. You'll find it's a lot easier to adjust water with wet hands. This is true for all magic unless it's directly bloodline related."

"Right…" I muttered. I stepped forward nervously. Until now, I'd never really been afraid of drowning. An image of me at the center of a floating ball of water I'd made but couldn't escape popped into my mind. I shook my head and hands nervously. "So… how exactly am I supposed to do this?"

"Concentrate," Saxe advised. "Because you're just starting out, why don't you say your suggestion out loud."

"Suggestion?"

"Yes, all of the best magicians never command something to happen; that's incredibly rude. Suggest it to rise or to speed back down the riverbed. Be creative."

I wondered if he knew just how crazy he sounded. He spoke so highly of inanimate things. I wondered vaguely if that was my own future. I could just picture myself as an old man kneeling beside a stream and laughing at its quiet jokes. I raised an eyebrow, hoping he was going to let me in on a joke or laugh at my gullibility. He gave me a reassuring smile and nodded to the stream. I felt ridiculous, but I did it anyway. I dipped my hand into the stream and asked nicely for the water to jump a little. I saw no result.

I tried again and again. Each time, I added something else. A new tone, a different rhythm, an unusual movement.

After the hundredth time, I threw my hands up with a dramatic sigh. "Nothing's working!" I exclaimed.

"No, that's not quite true." My hopes rose a little. "I think a pebble moved that last time." My hopes came rushing back down again.

I groaned again. "Why not skip the middleman and focus on the pebble?"

Saxe crossed his arms and gave me a disappointed

look. "Are you ready to give up so soon?"

I huffed but took the suggestion. My fingers were still dripping, so I didn't feel the need to get it wet again. I closed my eyes and reached out my hand. I might have imagined it; it was almost as if I felt the water moving beside me. Again, I asked it to jump up. And I used please this time. I slowly closed my open palm into a fist and jerked upward. At first, I noticed no difference, so I dropped my fist to my side and relaxed my fingers. Just as I opened my eyes again, gallons of water fell on my head.

I spluttered and stumbled, trying to remember how to breathe. I tripped and fell right into the stream. The cold of the water rushing around me took my breath away. Smooth pebbles scattered beneath me as I bolted up and drew in a deep breath. I wiped the water from my face and blew my mop of hair out of my eyes. Glaring up at Saxe I said,

"Please, tell me that was you."

"No," he chuckled. "I'm afraid that was all you."

I couldn't help but notice that he was only splashed, while I couldn't have been wetter if I tried. I shook the water from my hair. "Great, I've always wanted to be a fish." The water around me gurgled in agreement. I stood up hesitantly, not wanting to be dissolved into bubbles or some other horrific death.

"Why don't you try something else?" He closed his eyes in frustration as I shook myself off like a dog. "If you think you can manage, we'll do wind. To help you dry off."

I stepped out of the stream and onto the muddy grass. "Do I do the same thing?"

"For the most part. The wind is more difficult. I have no doubt in my mind that you possess the power, but do you possess the strength to harness it?"

113

He gave me a long look. A look that I didn't quite catch the meaning of. I took a deep breath and closed my eyes. "This time, ask the air around you to bring the water out of your clothes," he instructed. "Last time, you didn't make a sound. You called out from your mind. Perhaps that's the key for you: to do it mentally."

I was aware of how foolish that sounded. If the air heard everything, I thought, then it would know just where I thought this whole world could go. I sighed and closed my eyes again. I stretched my hand directly above my head and balled my hand into a fist.

I'm not sure why a fist, but it felt right. Saxe hadn't given me any kind of clue on what to do with my hands. I was improvising, and that almost always worked. As I slowly brought my hand down, I spread out all of my fingers, asking the wind to do the same with the water in my shirt. It felt like gentle fingers were plucking the water from me. Once my hair and clothes were dry, I asked the wind to send the water they'd taken off me and put it back in the stream. I cracked one of my eyes open and saw a shower of individual droplets of water dropping back into the river they'd come from.

A rush of exhilaration came into my body. I grinned uncontrollably. I wanted to keep working at it, so I asked the wind to take the extra water I'd dumped on the grass and put it back too. I felt the excess water glide out from the puddle I stood in. An arc of water caught the sun in a rainbow of refracting colors. I had both of my eyes open now, and I wanted to try something that I knew the old man beside me would probably disapprove of. "Pick me up, please," I asked in my mind.

My bare toes had a death grip on the grass. As I rose shakily into the air, I scrambled to keep contact with the earth. Stalks of grass remained clamped between my toes as I hovered for a moment, I trying to get my bearings. I leaned left and the wind adjusted to let me drift left. I did a slow flip and the world turned with me, leaving me dizzy and disoriented. Blinking the stars from my eyes, I smiled as another spontaneous idea came to me. I put my feet together and pushed forward. I zoomed around the apple tree. The wind ran through my hair, and my smile stretched across my entire face. Beaming, I touched back down beside him.

"How was that?" I asked, breathless.

He looked at my dried clothes and wind-ruffled hair. "Are you sure you've never studied anywhere else?"

"Pretty sure, but my clothes say otherwise." I began inspecting myself. "It would have taken me forever to dry them out normally. That was incredible."

"Yes, but a master of the elements could have gone

around the tree much faster." He raised his eyebrow at me doubtfully. We shared a look. A ghost of a smile appeared on his face before he walked towards his garden.

I laughed and hurried after him. "What now?"

"You pull weeds from my garden."

"What? What happened to 'Cole, you must practice today. You've been here for days and haven't shown any interest in magic!' Now I'm pulling weeds?" I'd done my best impersonation of him I could, which might have offended him, but it gave me an idea. "Say! Is there magic I could learn to change my appearance?"

"Yes."

I asked the wind to help me, and I drifted forward to keep up with him. "Is that a lesson we're learning soon?"

"No."

"Why not?" I touched down in front of him. I had to

run backward to see his face as he walked swiftly towards the cottage. His cloak ruffled in the breeze. "Eventually, I'm going to need to leave, and those thugs from the market might recognize me. I'll need a pretty good disguise."

"Changing one's appearance and surroundings is a clue to someone's intentions. Someone who focuses on that is only up to mischief and has evil intentions." He paused in front of his garden. "Best to steer clear of them."

I nodded slowly. Wanting desperately to change the subject, I nodded to the overflowing garden. "So are these magical herbs?"

"No, you just stepped on my basil."

I backed up, careful not to step on anything else.

"Call out to the soil in your mind. Ask it to send minerals and water to the plant you stepped on."

I scooped up a little dirt and smashed it into my

hands. I looked down at the dark stains on my hands. How foolish did I look? I steeled myself for future ridicule and took a deep breath.

I asked the plant to straighten back up and be plentiful for the lonely wizard. With my palm open, I slowly moved my hand upward. It felt like I was lifting a thousand pounds with it. When I opened my eyes, the plant had straightened and sprouted many new leaves, but so had every other plant in the garden. The crowded garden was way too small to contain all of it.

Saxe looked like he wanted me to think he was pleased, but I could tell he was worried. "Right," Saxe said slowly. He bent down and plucked a mint leaf the size of his hand. He turned it over and inspected it. "Impressive." He began tearing the leaf into smaller pieces to seep for tea. "Let's not try fire... Just in case." He paused, studying me.

If we weren't going to do fire, the lesson was nearly over. With the hand that was behind my back, I made a fist. I imagined floating in front of the window that overlooked the garden. I knocked on the open air and heard a very faint rapping on the window panes. Saxe turned around to investigate. I knew Lyla would need time to descend the stairs, so I improvised.

"Sir, do you specialize in a particular element?" I asked.

"No, but I've practiced and gotten better at all of them."

"Even the element of-" I appeared on his other side with my newfound flying skill, "surprise?"

"Sort of."

"Then what do you consider yourself to be especially good at?"

"Come, I'll show you." He walked briskly across the field, and I had to run to keep up with him. He walked quickly through the kitchen and up the stairs. I fell behind and peered into our bedroom. Lyla was lying on her bed, reading a poetry book. If I didn't know any better, I would say she had been there for hours. She gave me a wink and returned to her reading as though nothing had happened.

I smiled softly before following him up the stairs and to his study. I hesitated in the doorway. He was inspecting his desk. He looked up when I walked in and a grim smile haunted his face. He closed and locked the door, even though no one was downstairs but Lyla. He waved his arms around the room, casting spells and charms to soundproof the room.

I watched him as curiosity mounted in me. He finished at the window, with his back to me. He turned slowly as if he were afraid to face me. "Sit."

I hesitantly sat. Given how Saxe was acting, I expected fire to shoot from the walls or lightning to strike me dead.

He pulled out the chair from his desk and sat facing me. He placed his elbows on his knees and rested his chin on his fingers. "You've shown significant signs of promise in all the elements," he said.

I laughed halfheartedly. "You have the power of observation?"

"No," he hesitated, weighing his following words carefully. "I have the gift of prophecy," he paused, waiting for a reaction.

I blinked, waiting for proof.

"I've seen many wonderful and terrible things happen. Sometimes I see things years in advance, other times just mere minutes. I can intervene and help those affected before it happens most of the time. Sometimes there's nothing I can do but watch. After a while, it does get hard to sort out the real from the… not so real. So I write everything down." He gestured to his bookshelves.

I laced my fingers and pressed two fingers to my lips. I nodded slowly, expecting Saxe to continue. Something about this felt strange. A tingle of déjá vu ran its fingers down my back.

I was still confused. "What does that have to do with me?"

He picked up a thick, leather-bound book with four symbols on the cover. "I was hoping you'd ask that. Why not start where every story does? At the very beginning."

# Chapter Six:

## Studious Me

I took the book and retreated into the quiet of the bedroom Lyla, and I shared. I closed the door but left the window open. Sometime during our discussion, Lyla had abandoned the room for the front yard. If I craned my neck out the window, I could see her silhouette dancing alone through the tall grass. She gathered flowers and weaved grass jewelry. She was so content being alone, so comfortable in her imagined world. I knew I would have enough time to start a chapter before lunch.

I desperately wanted to know what Lyla had found, but my fingers itched to open the cover of this book. I longed to hear the crack of the spine and feel the pages between my fingers.

I sat down heavily on my bed, causing the mattress to groan and the bed frame to squeak. It all seemed too good to be true. Too wild to be authentic. The bed seemed too soft to spend too much time in it. How strange was it to think that only last month I had no idea where my next meal would come from. Only last year, we had barely scraped together enough to barter our way across the Mine Lick Creek. Now we had time to spare. I was *reading*, for heaven's sake. I'd always assumed reading was the hobby of decrepit old women and spoiled rich men.

The idea of opening the book and aging fifty years from mere boredom popped into my head. I slid off the bed and sat on the floor, leaning against the bedpost. "Chapter one…" I mumbled under my breath. I flipped to chapter one and found it was all handwritten notes. The chapter title page looked like it was added afterward.

"Chapter one," I read, "Magical Movements." I leaned back against the bed and set the book across my knees. The instructions were laid out in his lopsided handwriting:

Learning magic's movements is like memorizing a dance. The more complex the magic, the more complicated the steps.

For most magic, the magician needs a stimulant. To move oceans, you need only a single drop. Fire benders need only a spark to begin a full blaze. Earth elementalists need a mere handful of dirt to start growing a forest. However, for air, the magician requires patience. Although the air is all around them, the wind is finicky. It tends to ignore lesser wizards for its own will.

To begin manifesting magic, close your eyes and imagine moving the element of your choice. Start small. If it is water, you need to be able to hear the dripping of water into a pool in your hand. If you chose fire, picture the flickering flames of a match. Hear the crackle and popping of the wood underneath. Feel the heat emanating from it. If you chose earth, smell the rich soil, feel the moist dirt between your fingers. Hear the soft squish under your feet. If you mistakenly select wind, pray to your deities. Study the natural movements, then ask it to do the opposite. Feel the gentlest of breezes to the harshest of tornadoes.

Get a stimulant. Almost all magicians will need a stimulant. A stimulant will trigger the magic all creatures hold within them. Some magicians have the capability for only one type of magic. However, most have options to widen their scope.

A note was scribbled beside that paragraph that

mentioned bloodline magic not needing a trigger. Another note promised further explanation in later chapters but never specifically said where.

Next, let your arms hang freely at your sides. Every inch of your being should be relaxed. Raise your desired hand towards the water, fire, or earth source. Ask it politely to shift in an otherwise unnatural way. Allow your hand to do whatever motion is required for your action. A sweeping hand, a clenched fist, an open palm, or many more. In return for listening, offer it help. Supply the water with the magic to rise or the enchantment for your match's tiny flame to grow."

There was a note scribbled in the margin that read. "More details in chapters five through eight.

On the shelf under the window sill, several books resided. A small potted plant stretched into the sunlight.

Beside it, a cup of water sat. I crossed to Lyla's beside and peered inside the cup. A few gulps of water swirled in the bottom. I dipped a finger into the water and placed the cup carefully on back on the shelf. I closed my eyes and tried to relax as I backed up several paces. I reached out, looking for the water then imagined my finger in the cup again. The cool touch of water. The swooshing sound it made when the cup tilted. The rough-hewn edges of the clay contrasted with the smooth water. I asked it to rise gently. I allowed my pinky finger to move upward, then I forced my other fingers to follow in a wave. I jerked my hand upward.

I tensed when a crunch sounded. I squinted at the cup with one eye to find that the mug had split down both sides. Four pieces of clay lay in scattered pieces. Two on the table, two in random positions on the floor. I dropped my hands. This was so much harder than I had anticipated. How had I accidentally moved the entire stream earlier? How did I fill Saxe's garden with sprouts without meaning to? What was different about right now?

I shut the book with a sharp snap. Why couldn't I recreate my success? I was no closer to figuring out the secret that haunted River Haven.

I wanted to be angry with Saxe, with this mystical magic, with my odd circumstances, but I wasn't. I was only frustrated with myself. I could do this. I knew I could. I just had to keep trying.

I cautiously opened the book again. Saxe had intentionally directed me to chapter one, but this whole book was on magic. Perhaps there were parts he had written about in here that he was hoping I would never find. I leaned closer to the pages and began flipping through them, looking for anything suspicious.

"Air. Fire. Water. Earth." I flipped through those chapters without reading much. There were notes and sketches of people or hand motions along the margins of these chapters, but none of them helped me. I also skipped through the chapter titled 'Augur'. I didn't know how to pronounce it, let alone know what it was. I was increasing in speed as I flipped through the pages.

"Cole?"

I slammed the book shut and nearly jumped out of my skin. I tried to steady my heartbeat and breathing.

Lyla smiled at me. With one hand, she held her staff; with the other, she gingerly carried a dozen wildflowers blooming in their peak. "What are you doing?" she asked.

"Just... looking for something."

She busied herself with putting the flowers in a vase. She pretended not to notice the broken clay scattered around the room. "Have you tried the table of contents?"

I paused, "The what?"

She set her flowers gently on the bed and came to sit beside me. "It's at the front of every book, so you can find what you need." She flipped back to the front. "See? It has page numbers and everything."

She left it with me and got up to arrange her flowers.

I let my finger drift down the page. I flipped to the next page and did the same thing. My finger stopped on the page that was titled 'The End'. It carried a dark and ominous meaning. Even the ink seemed darker, fresher, newer. I flipped to the page number listed beside the title. There was still half the book to go; this couldn't possibly be the end of the book.

"Cole, should we talk about what I found?" she

whispered.

My heart raced as I ran my fingers across the ink on the table of contents. "Oh, maybe later."

"You don't want to know now?"

"We will talk… in private."

She took a deep breath. "I'm going to go help Mr. Saxe make lunch. I think it'll be ready in just a couple minutes."

I nodded deafly. I was staring at the title page. All the other title pages had sketches of whatever the chapter contained. This one had 'The End' written plainly on the page. Unlike the rest of the book, the pages were not worn from being reread. It seemed like he had written this and refused to reread it.

Lyla watched curiously, but I didn't say a word. She silently walked out of the room, quietly evaluating me the whole way. Once she was gone, I flipped the page to read the description:

A wizard's death is a gruesome and ugly thing. Even if a witch has spent her whole life helping the poor and needy, she will meet an unholy end. I have studied magic's history for years but cannot find a pattern to explain this.

The only reason I have obtained is this: magic is not meant to be in this world. Fate is angry with whoever dabbles in it. With magic, history can be rewritten, laws can be destroyed, cities and empires may fall, and even destiny itself has little power over it.

I fell into magic long before this discovery, but even at the beginning, I knew it was not for the faint of heart. I beg you, reader of this journal, to consider the repercussions of your actions."

I shut the book as fast as I could. My heart pounded in my ears, and my breathing was accelerated. Who knew reading could cause heart problems? Saxe thought this was dangerous enough to write a warning but not perilous enough to write it at the beginning? Why hadn't the warning been on the very first page? I flipped past the table of contents and to the very first page. I had neglected to read there, and in bold black ink, a warning was labeled.

Dangerous information disclosed inside. Read with care.

Why was I this blind? I couldn't help but smile frustratedly at my own faults. How valid was the warning? Had he put that there just to scare me? Was any of it true? Did I want to weigh the opportunity to learn a little magic for a little bit of risk? What was I saying? I knew myself well enough to know that death itself would have to stare me in the face before I changed my mind about some things.

Still, I had to think about my choices. I didn't want to die, as most men don't. But what scared me more than the thought of whatever void lay beyond this one was the thought that only one of us would go. I especially don't want to leave Lyla alone here. This despicable world would crush her if I didn't shelter her from it. I wanted to flee. I wanted to take my chances with the thugs, to escape this web of dangerous secrets, before it was too late. Would Saxe even let us leave?

I threw the book on my bed, hating myself. I didn't *want* to leave. River Haven was beautiful, secluded, and safe. But above all of that was an unimaginable hope. Magic lived and breathed here. I was drawn to it like a moth to a flame. A small part of me still believed I could make a difference by learning even a little bit of magic. I was thirsty for knowledge, and Saxe knew all. He already had a hook in me, now all he had to do was slowly reel me in. Before I knew it, I would be just another wizard, barreling towards inevitable death.

I sat on my hands, trying to list out all the reasons not to continue. But even as the list of potential evils grew longer, a little persuasive voice in the back of my head whispered, "Just finish the chapter." I slowly reached back and grabbed the spine. I slid it over the quilts and sheets and towards me.

My hatred for myself grew as I slipped my fingers under the cover and flipped to the right page. "Reading about magic doesn't make you a magician," I told myself. "You're still safe." I could lie to myself all I wanted, but deep down, I knew I was already marked for death.

There was a space beneath the paragraph I had already read. I flipped the page. It was blank. I let the page fall, covering the written words I had already read.

Written in small, straight, script was only three sentences:

I know this warning will do nothing to stop a determined young witch or wizard. As long as you are positive of your choice, it is my solemn duty to prepare you for the coming war. My hopes fly with you.

He knew? How could he have known? I didn't know myself.

I stretched my sleeping legs. I was going to get to the bottom of this. I just didn't know what that knowledge would cost me.

# Chapter Seven:

# My Element

I slid a finger under the page. "Soups on!" Lyla yelled. I jumped. I took a deep breath and told myself it was silly for me to feel the forces of darkness hurling around my small bedroom. I walked sullenly into the kitchen, wanting to get to the end of the chapter. Lunch passed slowly. The instant the conversation lulled, I tried to slip away. Saxe made some excuses about my practice. The rest of the day, he hovered nearby and I could never get away. It was as if he knew. But how could he?

Night fell, and still, I hadn't finished it. Finally, I saw the last of the old wizard. He smiled and said goodnight before trudging up the stairs. I hopped up and shut the door. In the darkness of our tiny bedroom, I smiled to myself. I laid back on my bed but didn't cover myself with a sheet. I waited eagerly for the chance to pull the book out from under my pillow.

"Goodnight, Lyla," I said as I rolled over.

She didn't answer, so I assumed she was already fast asleep.

I sat back up; all dreariness drained from me. I lit a candle with the matches from the bedside table drawer. I pulled the book out again.

Staring at the worn cover, I realized I didn't have the heart to face the end in darkness. What about the daunting future made it impossible to read without the chirp of birds and warmth of sunlight? I could feel a pressing evil. An evil I could never fight in the mystery of nightfall. I would have to wait until the morning after all. I was angry at my own cowardice but still couldn't manage to read the end.

"Why aren't you finishing it?"

It was Lyla. I turned to look at her. She had rolled over to look at me.

"I know you've been eager to finish it all day, so why aren't you?"

I sat up and put the book on my nightstand. "I… don't know," I admitted.

"I think I do." She rolled onto her back. She stared at the ceiling instead of meeting my eyes. "It doesn't take Mr. Saxe to figure that out." I gave her a questioning look. "I know you're more scared than you let on. You put up this shield when you know people are watching. You have your guard up until you think you're alone. The moment you believe you're alone, you look terrified." She took a deep breath and turned to look at me.

I opened my mouth to protest, but she wasn't

finished. "I know you think you're helping me by being strong or something, but you aren't. In fact, you've been doing this my whole life. The day Mom and Dad died, you stepped into the giant shoes of my guardian. From misadventure to disaster, you kept up your brave face. But did you really think I couldn't see right through it?

"The only thing you're proving is that you don't trust me. I thought, for a second, that maybe you trusted me enough to let me search Mr. Saxe's study on my own. Yet, here we are again. I get to watch you fall apart and stitch yourself back together again with a smile and a laugh. All for the sake of what exactly? Pride?"

I took a deep breath and tried to sort out my thoughts. "Maybe more like humanity?" I slung my legs over the bed, so I was looking directly at her. "I didn't want you to see me afraid or hurting because I didn't want you to feel that way. I know it didn't quite do that, but I wanted to shield you from the world as long as I could." I took a staggering breath and looked at her staff beside her bed. I hung my head in failure when I saw her still legs again.

"I understand," she said, reaching for her staff. She padded softly over to me and climbed into bed with me. "But could you tell your inner Atlas it's time to share the burden a little bit?"

A small smile spread across my face. I nodded.

She crossed her legs and sat the staff across her lap. "So, now can I tell you what I saw?"

I rolled my eyes. "Tell me before you burst."

"He had shelves upon shelves of books up there. I knew I couldn't search everywhere, so I started with the desk. Lots of notes in different languages or in a code. A few hazy sketches and the title 'We Met in the Fog'. There was a notebook on his bedside table that-"

"Wait, wait, wait! Bedside table? You went into his room?" I laughed as her face reddened.

"On accident," she explained, "but I thought, while I was there, why not look around?"

"A good point, I guess."

"Anyway, there was something in there about an 'Augur'. I figured out what it meant a little later when you were at another lesson."

"You mean you've read this book?" I gestured to the book on my nightstand.

"Only the table of contents. Oh, and Chapter 18."

"Lyla-"

"No further than that. Just enough to learn what it was. And I might have been the least bit curious." She saw my expression and turned away with a mischievous smile.

"Turns out, an Augur is someone who can see the future."

"Like Saxe?"

"Exactly. Most of the chapter was hypothetical. Almost a scientific journal. There was also a slip of paper in there." Lyla pulled a slip of paper out of a pocket somewhere deep in her nightclothes. "It's a sketch."

"You just happened to have that on you?"

"I thought he might find it if I put it on the table or in a drawer. I'm not crazy."

"Crazy prepared," I murmured.

She playfully hit my shoulder. She spread it out on my bedsheets. Four silhouetted people held hands. Wait a minute, the one on the left wasn't holding anyone's hand. Was that supposed to signify the rebel? The one on the far right was thin and scrawny; he held out beside him a walking staff identical to the one Lyla now held.

I paused. What was that supposed to mean? If Saxe was so confident I was a part of this, why did I have Lyla's staff? Or was that Lyla holding the walking stick? Was she involved too? The idea sent shudders through me. I took a deep breath and studied the rest of the picture.

The other three had no identifying figures. They were blurred and disproportionate, so I couldn't even tell their gender.

"It's not much," Lyla admitted. "But it's something."

"Did you see anything else?"

"He had a pixie on his bookshelf."

"I noticed that too."

"Most of his books are about the past, past dictators, fallen kingdoms, and such. All of his journals are filled with tiny glimpses of the future. He has an entire shelf full of notebooks that are signed and dated with every vision he ever received."

"And?"

"Apparently, he's seen us coming for a while. He's seen every step it took to get here. From Leangap to Long Hollow to Carlin. He's seen it all."

A flash of hot anger washed over me. "And he didn't think to help us out a little? If he was aware of it all, then where was he? Why didn't he help us when we were starving in Big Bottom? Where was he when I was whipped for hours in Leangap? Or all those other times the world turned its back on us?"

"He did help us. A diversion in Leangap so you could get away. A dropped coin in Big Bottom. A protective hand when we passed over Eagle Creek. He was there with us through all of it."

"Then why wait until now to remove us from

dangerous situations? We've been hurt plenty before we got to Carlin."

She dropped her voice. "Mr. Saxe was preparing us for something."

"For what?"

She gathered herself and slid off the bed. She shrugged. "You know more about the prophecy than I do." She laid down in her bed and gingerly put her staff beside her bed. "Goodnight, Cole. Sleep well."

"Goodnight, Lyla." I doubted I would get much sleep. I stared at the ceiling until I heard her breathing deepen. I rolled over and grabbed the book again. The world around me seemed to darken at the thought of facing the end. I couldn't sleep, and I did not dare finish the book.

I didn't have any dirt or water, and I wasn't willing to try fire. Air seemed difficult from the description. *Just practice the hand motions,* I thought. I set the book in front of me and studied the sketches. I mimicked the pictures and moved through them several times.

I closed my eyes and did it from memory. I pictured the room around me. Every inch of open air was there in my mind. As an experiment, I focused on the air section by the door. The book had said to ask for something unnatural. *Could you please turn a different color?* I asked. I focused and tried to stretch my magic that way. I scrunched up my eyes, hoping it would comply.

I opened my eyes to find a floating blob of purple. I moved my hand, and the mist rolled as well. I had actually done it.

Excitement flooded me as I stood up. After so much searching, I had found my element. The air was not confined by rules, boundaries, or authority. The wind flew wherever it wanted. It was free, just like me.

It bounced around the room and never lost its color. Eventually, I allowed it to drift out the window and into the waiting darkness.

I had done it. I'd actually done something magical. This might mean I was deeper into magic than I had initially thought. The warning of a wizard's death still pestered me. But I was too excited to worry about it too much. I couldn't wipe the smile from my face. This was a baby step; maybe soon, I would move boulders or change weather patterns.

The thrill of my discovery was still coursing through me. I celebrated silently by jumping up and down, allowing the wind to bear most of my weight. Lyla was still asleep next to me. My toes touched back down on the threadbare rug, my head began to swim. I clasped a hand to the bed, trying to steady myself. Had I overexerted myself? Was this because of the magic I had just performed? I felt myself falling, but I couldn't move any of my body to catch myself. My vision faded, and I lost touch with the world I knew.

A different world came into focus. A better world. A world where all was well.

It was dark. I could feel grass swaying around me. I was lying on my back, looking up at the millions of stars. Lyla was asleep on my shoulder. The birds were sleeping, and so was the sun. The moon was so prominent in front of us. It chased all the darkness away from our little valley.

A rustle of movement caught my attention from the western portion of the valley. I inched Lyla off my shoulder and stood up, wary of coming danger.

The darkness took the form of a person, no taller than I was. They looked thin, malnourished, and angry. The character's face was shadowed and hazy. I stood my ground over Lyla. Each step the person took sent shivers down my spine. I knew this person was dangerous, but terrifyingly enough, I didn't know why.

They radiated hatred. So much so, I could feel myself absorbing the aura. I wanted to fight him. I wanted to win.

I began running forward. The shadowy figure charged as well. I jumped upward and allowed the wind to hurl me forward. Just as the sun's first rays crested over the hilltop, I whipped my hand straight, sending a magic spear of wind his way. The sun blinded me before I could strike. All was bright and formless.

I hit the floor hard.

I lay on the floor with my arms and legs tangled from my fall. Through the uncomfortable silence, I could hear my hard breathing. I opened my eyes slowly. Lyla was peering down at me.

Where was I?

Lyla smiled, "Are you okay, Cole?"

I sat up quickly, looking for the person. The sun wasn't even up, but the sky was brightening. How was that possible? Hadn't it just been dark only moments before? I turned and saw the intricately carved door absorbing the sunlight's rays nearby. We were at River Haven. I laid back down in relief and put my hands on my face.

"Yes," I sighed, "fine."

"You were mumbling again."

"What did I say?"

"My name a few times, the number four, and another word I couldn't catch."

"Did I wake you up?"

She didn't answer.

"I'm sorry, Lyla, I didn't mean to wake you."

She smiled. "It's fine. Will you hand me my crutch?"

I leaned over and grabbed the walking stick. I vaguely wondered if everyone could see the faint blue light. Why wasn't she amazed by it like I was? She slung her legs over the bed and tip-toed towards the door. She inched it open and waved for me to follow.

Had I scared her into leaving River Haven? Was it really that easy?

We walked silently down the hall and through the kitchen. The kitchen vines and flowers were in full bloom. I expected the old man to be awake making tea and studying by candlelight, but he was nowhere to be found.

She led me up the hill and to the apple tree. We climbed until the branches thinned out and became slender and gave under our weight.

"What are-"

She held a finger to my lips and pointed over the horizon. "Shh, you'll ruin the magic."

Magic?

She pointed to the eastern horizon. As I watched, mother nature in all her beauty unfolded. Rays of sunlight shot across the sky, filling the air with radiant majesty. The clouds burned with soft pinks and vibrant purples. The valley was overrun with light, where darkness had ruled only a moment before.

Only last night, I had marveled in amazement at my small feat of magic. But now I knew what true power was. And I didn't have to work or try to behold it; it gave itself freely to anyone willing to watch.

"Magic," Lyla repeated.

"Magic," I agreed. I turned to look her full in the face. She gripped her staff in one hand and a tree branch in the other. She smiled warmly.

"How often do you come out here?"

She blushed. "Most mornings."

"But you are always asleep when I get up."

"That's because I stay out here for a little while then go back to bed."

"Not sure if our host would approve." I smiled.

She turned back to the horizon and shrugged. "Rules never really were our forte, were they?

# Chapter Eight:

# Strange Dreams

We sat perched like eagles on the top of the apple tree as the sun continued to rise. We chatted and laughed like we had before we came to River Haven, before the accident, before we met Saxe. My heart ached as I counted the days since our last tender memory. It had been too long. I opened my mouth to comment on it when a tea kettle began to whistle.

We turned in unison back towards the cottage. With one last glance at the now risen sun, we wordlessly started climbing down. Lyla was just above me and periodically jumped down a branch, scattering leaves down on me. I was on the last bough and preparing to sling down when she dropped down past me. She landed in a crouch and looked up at me with a mischievous twinkle in her eye.

I dropped down beside her. "Want to- "

She took off running. I scrambled to catch up with her. She ran with one hand clutching the staff, but she didn't seem to need it for support. The healing magic emanating from it was enough to keep her standing.

"Hey!" I yelled after her, "You cheated!"

She turned, sprinting backward now. She shrugged. "What can I say? I learned from the best!" She laughed and turned around just in time to bolt through the waiting door of the cottage.

I dug my heels into the ground and skidded to a stop. I had caught sight of Saxe through the kitchen window. Even though the glass, I could tell he was watching me. He had a strange mix of emotions on his face. It was contorted with sorrow but also a blend of joy.

He still had secrets, and it was my job to bring them to light.

I walked into the kitchen just as Saxe was pouring Lyla and me a cup of tea. A vast array of breakfast items awaited us.

How had he gotten all of this done? He was not in here when Lyla and I snuck through earlier.

Nevertheless, the biscuits steamed, and the gravy was hot. A glass of orange liquid was set in front of me. "What's this?" I asked, leery of poisons and potions.

"Orange juice," Lyla piped up.

"The juice of oranges? How long did it take you to squeeze them all?"

"Not long."

"Is there a spell for that?"

"No, it's just science."

"Science and magic coexist?"

"Well, what is science but a modern form of magic?"

I took a hesitant sip of the stuff. I wrinkled my nose as the acidic juice ran down my throat.

"You don't like it?"

"It's just different from rainwater, that's all."

I noticed that she had downed nearly an entire cup. When Saxe had his back turned, I poured mine into her cup.

She smiled deeply. Saxe glanced over his shoulder. I pretended to drink the last drop of my juice. "Can I get a refill? Maybe just water this time?"

He picked up a copper pitcher and poured ice-cold water into my cup. I sipped on the water and watched him work at the oven. "I trust you slept well?" he said.

"Yes," I lied.

Lyla gave me a sideways glance. Her expression conveyed that she believed our discussion about forwarding honesty should extend to everyone, not just her. I disagreed wholeheartedly. While there were a few things she didn't need to know, there were many things Saxe didn't need to know. One of which was my odd dream and the strange way it came to me.

His eyes shifted from hers to mine. "I don't believe you," Saxe said, raising his eyebrows before turning around again to put the kettle back on. "Is there anything I can help with?"

"No," I said, "just some strange dreams."

His back stiffened. I saw him take the pot off the heat before snuffing out the fire with one hand motion. It imploded with a puff of smoke. "What kind of dreams?"

"Strange ones."

Lyla's mouth lifted into a smile momentarily, but Saxe didn't find my repetition funny.

"What was the plot line?"

"Of my dreams? They don't make any sense!"

He turned around, "Why are you avoiding my questions?"

"Why do you care so much?"

He stared intently at me. If I didn't know any better, I might have thought he was trying to read my mind.

Lyla looked at me in fear. "Mr. Saxe, he was muttering about me and the number four."

"Thank you," he said kindly, but his eyes shone with worry.

He nodded absentmindedly and turned to me. "Cole, I'd like to speak with you privately."

I looked at Lyla. She looked as confused as I did.

Her surprise mingled with no small amount of hurt.

"We can't speak here?"

"There is something I'd like to show you."

I looked at Lyla again. She gave me a nod and a small smile. I stood up slowly and allowed him to lead me up the stairs to his study. He sat me down in the same chair I sat in when I arrived.

Was it my imagination, or did he look exhausted? Dark bags hung under his eyes, and his shoulders drooped to fit the frame of the chair. His beard wasn't tended to this morning, and his hands had a slight tremor. Every few minutes, he blinked hard as if reminding himself to stay awake.

"Sir, are you alright?" I asked, leaning forward carefully.

He shifted to look me in the eyes. "Cole, I need you

to tell me exactly what you saw."

Exasperated and worried for his health, I said, "But it was just a dream! It's not important!"

He shook his head, "No, it was a vision. A glimpse of a possible future."

I shuddered. Was that all really going to happen? Would I really have to fight someone like that? Who was the person?

"So, I'm begging you, tell me what you saw!"

I got an idea. "Let me show you." I closed my eyes and waved my hands around. I added trees and grass to my vision. A shadowy version of my dream played out when I opened my eyes. I saw the silhouettes of myself and Lyla lying in the grassy valley. The trees around us rustled as my attention was drawn to the hilltop. The person appeared as I rose.

We charged, but a blinding flash made my image disappear just before we collided. I sat back down heavily.

"You've improved dramatically," he commented, almost to himself, stroking his beard.

"I've been practicing at night while Lyla's asleep."

"Any notable reason for those particular hours?"

I shook my head slowly, carefully, as if not to scare a predator. "Waiting for a big reveal, I guess."

"Cole, will you do something for me?"

This was my chance. If I could bargain for information, we could finally make heads or tails of this place. All the questions I had thought in the past weeks flitted through my mind. "Only if you tell me what the foreseen four is and why you wanted me to stay here. Why did you leave us to suffer for most of our lives only to save us in the alley? And while we're bartering, where did you learn all of this?"

I knew I had asked for too much, but if I asked for too little, then our compromise could dwindle away all of my advantages.

He nodded and sat down. "Fair enough." He continued speedily as if he repeated the story a lot. "I learned from my father. Our family has always been magically inclined. I was blessed with the gift of prophecy. Or, more correctly, I was cursed with it. My brother resented me for it. You see, when a wizard dies, his most valued trait is passed down to his heir, and if the magic cannot find the desired heir, the man who killed him receives the power. My brother considered killing me because I had no heir, but he never succeeded. After years of dodging poisoned goblets and attacks while I slept, I left. I wasn't very old, but I needed a place to practice my craft in peace.

"So I plotted out River haven. I practiced my skills

and eventually built this cottage. I sowed each of the gardens and trees by hand. I strategically placed it here, between these high mountains. I could never be caught unaware if my brother ever brought an army into the valley.

"He never has. My knowledge has flourished here. I received a vision several years ago of a bright-eyed girl running ahead of a dark-haired boy. Both wore stolen clothes and ran laughing into town.

"I also saw that, unless I intervened, this would be the last happy day of the boy's life. The girl's life would end abruptly later the same day."

Saxe paused. When he continued, the calm and distant tone had left his voice. "I've grown quite fond of both of you. I can't imagine ever letting you leave, knowing that was your fate. However, if that is your wish, then you may do so."

I felt glued to my chair. How had I persuaded him to tell me all of this? Was the deal he was offering so crucial that he was willing to give anything anyway? What had I just walked into?

"I'm starting to think I should have asked for more. What's your deal?"

"You inform me, immediately, if you have another dream like this."

"How do I tell them apart from other dreams?"

"If it's about dancing chickens or chance meetings, then it doesn't hold long-standing importance. We can still talk about it, but it will not change the course of history. If it's about Lyla, or yourself, or is like the one we just witnessed, I beg you: tell me."

I had learned so much already, but he had left out the only piece of information I really needed. I leaned forward,

"Deal, but only if you tell me what the Foreseen Four is."

"We will discuss the Four if you agree to my deal."

He knew how to bargain and I was prepared to agree entirely. My words to Lyla echoed in my ears. What did I have to lose? I stuck out my hand, then I paused. *You*, Lyla, had said. She didn't want to lose me. Why did I feel the need to hesitate? It was just a dream, after all.

"Deal," I said. We sealed it with a handshake.

He was silent for a moment as I sat in the uncomfortable silence that surrounded the office.

"She's a lot like you, you know," he said softly.

I looked stiffly to the door and beyond to where I knew she would be playing. "How so?"

"She's listening at the door right now."

"She heard all that?"

"Of course not, this cottage is protected by magic,

but this room especially is bugged. She heard us talking about a new pillow."

I laughed. "Lyla will never believe that."

"No, but she didn't hear us either."

I couldn't wait any longer. The question bubbled up in me like lava about to explode. "So what are the Four?"

He sighed. "Why are you so eager?"

"All you've done is hide it from me! I want to know why it's such a big secret."

"It's your past, your future, your everything! Why can't you just live one more day in oblivion, one more day in the sun? This has eaten at me for years, and it may be years yet before it comes to pass. I don't want the weight of it on your young shoulders."

"Just tell me! Whatever it is, I can handle it. Lyla and I have been alone our whole lives. We almost died countless times. My entire life has been never-ending chapters of challenges and hardship. Whatever you think this is, just tell me. You can't scare me; you can't threaten me. Just tell me!"

He took a shuddering breath; it was as if the weight of it really had been crushing him. "Many years ago," he began. "I received a prophecy, a vision, involving four young people." He leaned forward, putting his elbows on his knees and staring intently at his hands. "They were best friends, high and low, good or bad, they stuck together. This vision foretold their coming betrayal. Unlike a typical friendship quarrel, this one would end in death. It will be a bloodbath. Each of the friends was versed in elemental magic. Either they kill the friend who betrayed them, or he kills them all.

"It was heartbreaking to watch, but even more so once I met a member of the coming horrors." With this, he looked up at me. There were tears in his eyes.

I froze, not sure what to believe. Why did this resonate with me? Did this sound familiar? Why was my heart racing? My hands were becoming restless. I stood up, suddenly scared of what he implied. "You think I'm involved in this?"

He dropped his head into his hands.

I smiled weakly. "Jokes on you; I have no friends." When I couldn't play off my nervousness, I stood up and began pacing. "Did you see who the traitor is?" I asked quietly after a moment of silence. Why was I so nervous all of a sudden? Why did this have to affect me?

He studied me carefully, "No."

I'd never had any real friends, but I'd made enough enemies to last me many lifetimes. Friends were not so different from enemies, right? Both required regular encounters. If too much time is spent apart, you begin to forget each other. From what I understood, you would tell stories about your interactions, from embarrassing moments to fights you shared. Strong emotions were always involved when remembering each other. A horrific thought came to me. "How do you know I'm not the rebel? I don't want to kill three people!" I ran my fingers through my hair in a nervous frenzy.

"I know." He was calm. How was he so quiet?

"So I am?" I whirled around on him. I stood in front of him, refusing to move, demanding answers.

"No." He laced his fingers together.

"You know for certain?" My fingers curled and uncurled nervously.

"Lyla," he said.

"Lyla," I repeated, nodding. Then paused, "What's

Lyla got to do with this?"

"You would do anything for her. Would a heartless monster do that? When I asked you what job you held, you said...?"

"Brothering," I finished. "So all of this," I gestured to the cottage and to the valley where we practiced. Angrily I stomped to the door and gestured to where my sister would be. "All of that was to train me to take down some rebel? What if I say no? We have nowhere to go. Will you cast us out? Will you keep us, prisoner? Would you hurt Lyla? Will you kill us since we know your dirty secrets?"

He shook his head sadly. "I've grown to love both of you. I couldn't bring myself to hurt a single hair on your heads."

I was touched, but my heart still pounded. I got up and began to pace. "But-but how? I don't have one friend, let alone four!"

"Cole, ordinarily, I see visions as if through water or smoke, always blurry and hard to decipher, never repeating. But this one," he shook his head sadly, "I have seen this every night since the moment I first received it. Every night it's the same. Every night, I suffer with those friends."

"How do I fit in all this?"

He heaved a heavy sigh and walked towards me. The love in his eyes was evident, but so was the fear and the amazement. "Because last night, I didn't have a vision."

"So maybe the future has changed. Crisis averted."

He placed his hands gently on my shoulders. "I think I unknowingly gave up my curse. Last night, I was sure of my fate. I finally chose an heir. Having no children of my own, I placed my gifts into someone else's hands. A boy who, much like me, was curious but deeply entwined in fate's master web."

"You made *me* your heir?"

He nodded.

"Why? You barely know me!"

Saxe shook his head before turning to lean on the mantle. "Cole, I feel as though I've known you a thousand lifetimes. You're the one. Sadly, you are also caught up in this net made of years of visions and studying. Each fiber is a pulsing, breathing thing that lives and changes daily. In the end, though, it always settles enough for the beginning battle scene."

I looked out the window, trying to calm my thoughts.

"I think your dream is the first of many ulterior perspectives of the same instance," he explained.

I ran my fingers through my hair and shut my eyes.

Now I could see why he was so hesitant to share the vision. I was a fool-hearted sheep. I let him lead me right into this trap of deception and magic. This whole place was a lion, ready to pounce on an unwitting victim. I knew the flowers smelled too sweet, the riverbed to inviting, the beds too soft to be true. Why had I played along as though nothing could go wrong?

He turned on me suddenly. "That is why it is of the utmost importance that you describe each dream to me in detail the moment they happen. If you wait too long, it could fade or change again. Can you promise me that you'll keep me in the know? Always?"

I faced him for the first time since he began walking around.

My heart was resolute. Lyla and I would leave the first chance we could. I took a deep breath, trying to calm the racing of my heart. Could I look straight into the eyes of the man who had saved my life, only to lie? Could I betray him? Could I even convince Lyla to leave?

I turned from the window. I looked right into those amber eyes and planted false hope. "I'll do what I can," I said quietly.

He smiled. "That's all I ask."

# Chapter Nine:

# Dreams Shape Reality

I escaped down the stairs and to my bedroom, making the excuse of studying. Lyla was there, waiting for me.

I pulled her inside and closed the door. "We're leaving. Tonight, at midnight. I'll explain when I can." I let go of her and bent down. "We'll need to move fast, so only pack necessities."

I could hear it in the uncertain way she moved that she didn't want to leave. She bent down beside me and handed me a shirt. "I trust you, Cole. But I pray that you reconsider."

She stood up and opened the door.

If only she knew the danger we were in. If only she

could see how long we had put off the impending doom about to wash over us.

We had to leave. I didn't know what other options we had.

. . .

We went to bed that night as usual. I promised Lyla I would wake her when it was time to go. We both knew neither of us would sleep tonight.

I lay on my back, staring up at the ceiling. Was that my imagination, or were the edges of my vision going dark? I was not going to fall asleep, not so close to our departure time. I sat up and blinked hard. But the darkness persisted and washed over me.

I ran up the hill as fast as I could. The long grass

ripped at my legs and kept tripping me. I tore past them and reached the top of the mountain.

He was waiting for me there. He threw a force of magic at me, knocking my feet out from under me. I was on the ground before I knew what hit me. He had a hand on my throat before I could scream. I heard someone shout my name. Both of our heads snapped toward the sound.

It was Lyla screaming. She called again, and I saw her running up the hill. I wanted to tell her to stay where she was, but I was pinned to the ground. The boy smiled at me before thrusting out a hand towards Lyla. She crumpled to the ground, and there was nothing I could do to stop it.

All became darkness, and the world faded back in. Crickets chirped in the background, a curtain fluttered in a silent breeze.

I bolted up out of bed. I was drenched in a cold

sweat and shaking with fear. All escape plans vanished the moment I realized that Lyla was in danger. I turned to look at her. She had dozed off, waiting for me to tell her when it was time.

My bare feet hardly made a noise as I dashed over the normally sun-soaked floorboards. I stood over Saxe for a moment, weighing the importance of my dream. I didn't want to disturb him, but I knew he would demand to hear my newest vision.

I gently shook his shoulder. The moment my finger was on him, he jumped. "What is it, my boy?"

"Another dream."

He guided me to the kitchen, a marvel of magic and wonder. Even in the darkness, the magnitude of magic was extraordinary. What I did with the furthest extents of my concentration couldn't hold a candle to this. He took me to the vast stone countertop in the very middle. The top was worn smooth from years of being in a river somewhere; now, it was the centerpiece of Saxe's kitchen. The vines underneath it formed a chair.

Despite the importance of this moment, I marveled at the magic in this one room. It was as though all the day things had gone to bed and left darker versions of themselves in their places. The flowers that bloomed in the night were composed of dark purples and deep blues; all were buds I don't remember seeing in the daylight. The moonlight streamed in through the open window, from which a cool spring breeze wafted.

He shook my shoulders to bring me back. "Cole, what's wrong?"

"Sorry, still tired, I guess."

"What did you see?"

Every time I closed my eyes, I saw Lyla falling. He was right about this knowledge being a burden. I already felt it pressing the life from me. "It's Lyla," I breathed.

His eyes grew wide.

I began the torture of picturing the thing I couldn't unsee. The image of Lyla's still body was imprinted on my eyelids. I closed my eyes and asked the air to help me. The magic leaked out of my fingers and into the air like a cold breeze was coming from the palm of my hands and floating into existence. I opened my eyes and watched mist flow from my fingers until a thick fog swirled around our feet. Closing my eyes again, I began molding the scene. The fog unfolded the scene around us like opening a book. I shaped Lyla as if from clay, then sent her into the picture. A miniature version of myself and the mysterious figure joined soon after. I put the doll size representations into play. The mist had started in a cloudy gray, which had been somewhat comforting yesterday. As the figure strangled me, a deep crimson corrupted the pictures. It was no longer fog, but smoke that burned my eyes and lungs.

I was pinned to the ground when she came running. I saw her draw closer and closer to danger while I struggled to fight off the assailant. The figure looked slowly from Lyla to me. I closed my eyes to avoid watching, but the vision continued playing in my mind.

It all swept together and disappeared with a dramatic swoop.

I took a deep breath once the smoke had cleared. "What does that mean?"

He wouldn't look at me. "It is set to change; nothing is set in stone," he assured me. His words should have been comforting, but his actions showed stress and chaos. He ran his fingers through his hair and leaned heavily on the table.

"What can we do to change it?"

He looked at me, wide eyes and full of fear.

"Nothing. We must let this take its course."

"*Take its course*?" I repeated. "This is my sister's future. Her life is on the line. You want to just stand by and let this happen?"

"No, I would do anything in my power to keep you *both* from harm, but there is nothing we can do. Not yet."

I didn't like how he lingered on both. Something about his word usage made me think I wasn't out of the woods yet. "What do you mean *yet*?"

"We can't help a thing that hasn't happened yet."

"Sure we can!" I protested. "It's called prevention."

"We can't prevent it without knowing what it is," he explained calmly. "These things just take time. We'll keep an eye on her, and on the future.

# Chapter Ten:

## Uncertain Times

Saxe smiled proudly at me. "Actually, you will be the one watching the future."

"What?" I jumped up. "Shouldn't something this important have more... experienced eyes watching?"

He smiled. "It's okay; call me old."

I smiled sheepishly as he continued.

"Since the day before last," he explained, "I haven't seen a single thing from the future. While sleeping, it is dark and formless. While awake, I see the world only as it is. I'm afraid you're the only asset we have."

I paused before responding. Every gear in my brain had shaken off the cobwebs of sleep and was moving at full speed. "Is that normal? For an heir to receive the gifts before the giver is..."

He nodded. "Go ahead, say it."

"Dead?"

"Quite the opposite. Highly unusual." He sat down heavily. "I am far from dead, despite what your young soul might think. However, my youthfulness is merely a facade. I am equally as far from life."

I came to stand beside him. "What do you mean?" I put a hand on his shoulder, sensing a growing burden on his shoulders.

"For weeks, I have been slowly losing all of my magical abilities."

"What!" I exclaimed.

Saxe hushed me and gestured to the room where Lyla slept. He slowly rose and walked to the front door. He opened it without a sound and stared up at the moon. He looked back at me and gestured for me to follow him. He disappeared out the door.

I gave Lyla's cracked bedroom door a quick glance. I hurried after him. He was lowering himself to sit at the base of the apple tree with no minor degree of difficulty. Every move seemed to pain him.

My feet soundlessly trotted across the soft grass. "Sir, please, let me help." He finally managed to plop himself down between the roots. "How could this happen? Why?"

He sighed and leaned toward me. I knelt down. Now that I wasn't looking down at him while he spoke, I could see the stress lines and dark circles under his eyes. "I suspect my brother, though I don't know how he's done it. Perhaps I am just getting old and am losing touch with reality." He patted the grass next to him.

I wanted to comfort him, but I wasn't sure what to

say. He was older than I was by at least twenty years, but he wasn't old enough to need half-moon spectacles and a silver beard that dragged the floor. His hair was graying and beginning to thin in some places. His beard was well tended to and had a deep chestnut color. His every movement radiated long-lasting life. How could all of that be erased with just a spell?

"He can do that?" I stammered. "Just kill you? With a spell?"

He shook his head. "No. Human life is valuable and too precious to end with a spell. My brother would have killed me long ago if that was an option. Magic can dwindle a person down to nothing but a shadow of what he once was, but it cannot be magic that kills him. Poison, suffocation, a knife, those can kill a man. But not magic."

"How is he doing this? Is he in River Haven?"

"To your second question, I can say no. Unless I am more limited than I originally realized. I would know if someone, especially my brother, stepped onto my land. To answer your first question, I'm not sure. Long-distance spells rarely last this long. He must be close enough and powerful enough to keep sending the effects my way. But he must have targeted me somehow. Normally, touch is required to start a curse like this. He must have found me while I was away. But when? Where?"

I felt like I was just listening to him think out loud. "What will happen to you if he does manage to get into River Haven?"

"Once he thinks I am incapable of helping myself, he will attack and kill me," he paused, "along with anyone near me."

I had previously been looking down at my feet,

hoping I never lived to see the day Saxe died. I had only known him a little while, but he had helped me more than any adult in my life until now. My eyes snapped up after hearing this. "We're in danger too."

He only nodded, but I knew there was more he wasn't saying.

"How long until he comes?" I asked, baiting him.

He still wouldn't meet my eyes. "I couldn't say. It could be a month, or it could be another hundred years."

"You're hoping the Four will come to pass before then?"

He looked up, and when he met my eyes, I saw tears glistening in them. "I don't think I can express how truly sorry I am for all of this. Fate is a fickle thing, and it is crueler to some people more than others." He stopped as emotion flooded him. He seemed so strong just the day before, but now his shoulders looked frail as they shook in the moonlight.

"What are you saying?" I turned to face him.

"No matter what path you choose, Cole, your life will not be a happy one for very long," he stopped and put a hand on mine. "I care for you both very much, so I set you on the one that would give you each the most time."

"Cut the riddles, Saxe. Tell me what you mean."

"Neither one of you will live to be my age." Shock filled my face, but anger was my first response. I clenched my fists and tried to bite my tongue. "I'm sorry," he said quietly.

I wanted to yell and scream at him. Apologies still flowed from his mouth, but I had tuned out every word. I flew straight up into the cover of the tree. I landed lightly on the top branch. He apologized again as I searched for a place to clear my mind. The woods behind the cottage caught my eye. He called my name and begged for forgiveness. I flew over his little house and touched down in the tree cover.

I began running. I let my brain's gears stop grinding for a moment while my legs pumped. My eyes focused only on what was directly in front of me. The rest of the world faded into my peripheral vision. I probably would have kept running if it weren't a perfectly placed pond.

I barreled through an area of tightly knit trees and tumbled right over the overhang. I plummeted into the pond with a giant splash. I came back up spluttering. A frog croaked nearby, almost as if it were laughing. I stumbled out of the pond, dragging up mud and plant muck as I did.

I plopped gloomily down at the edge of the pond. The flood of thoughts I had tried to keep at bay came rushing back in. I was drowning under the guilt and shame of leaving and the anger from the betrayal of Saxe. Should I go back? Should I try to escape with Lyla? Would she even want to come with me? I put my head in my hands.

I shoved my hands in my pockets and let one of my legs stretch until a foot rested in the water.

Who did he think he was to choose my future? He may have seen it coming, but I was the one who had to deal with the consequences.

Knowing the future was fun when there was nothing important coming. But the moment you were locked into a position like mine, you wished you'd never glimpsed it. I wish I had just kept my problems to myself and had never gotten tangled up in all of this magic business.

Then the next phase hit me. Grief.

I mourned for us. Lyla and I would die young. I would never get to watch her grow old, fall in love, or have children. There was no hope for improvement.

My back hurt, and my legs cramped from sitting

there for heaven knows how long, but I didn't have the strength or the motivation to move.

My life has never been simple. I had always sought simplicity but could never achieve it. I had thought life in a cottage by a stream would be closer to that dream. Add in magic, a prophecy, and a deranged wizard, and you have the exact opposite. Why couldn't something in my life be easily obtained, for once?

I kicked a stone into the water's edge. The ripples spread across the surface of the still water before slowly calming again. I picked up a rock and let the wind send it hurdling across the water's edge and into the trees on the other side. I flicked the water with my toe, enjoying the cool against the hot summer air. I threw another rock; this one hit a tree on the other side and ricocheted back into the pond.

I felt the wind pushing at my back, urging me

forward. "Stop it," I waved it away, still feeling sulky. It pushed harder, and my body shifted forward. "Quit! Can't you see I'm trying to be moody?" A gust of wind that belonged only in a hurricane rushed at me. My face hit the dirt, and I was doubled over in an awkward position. I sat up, and my back popped in weird places. The wind would pay for that one.

I stood up and stepped into the water, unsure of what to do. A sudden gust of wind shot me forward, and I toppled headfirst into the water. I sat up and shook the water from my hair.

"What was that for?"

It did it again.

"Are you trying to make a point?"

It pushed at me again, slightly slower this time. I was slowly dragged forward, gathering speed as I went. As I sped up, I came out of the water. Only my feet skimmed the surface. A smile spread across my face. The wind let go of me, and I plummeted into the water.

When I surfaced, it was silent as if it was waiting for an apology. "Okay, okay, I see your point. But let's do that again!"

I was skating across the smooth surface of the water. I laughed. It sped up, and I leaned forward. I adjusted my feet, trying to turn. I toppled back into the water. I stood up quickly.

I jumped up, and the wind pushed at my back. This time I balanced on my heels and kept my knees bent. I let myself lean back on the thousands of hands moving me forward.

It was an incredible feeling. I could see the outlines of rocks and fish under me, but I maneuvered around them. I leaned over and let my hand brush the surface as well.

I zoomed around the pond until I lost my balance and hit the water face first. I spluttered and gasped, but my smile never wavered.

I didn't let my fear of failure stop me from trying again. I kept coming back, loving the thrill of adventure and the hope of mastery I would never achieve. As the moon sank, I climbed steadily out of the water. I pushed the hair from my eyes and began walking back up to the cottage. Saxe and I had many things to talk about.

. . .

My hand hovered uncertainly by the door knocker. I hadn't decided anything. Or had I? I turned and looked back into the trees where I knew the pond was hidden. I smiled and walked inside.

When I didn't see him in the kitchen, I flew up the stairs and to the first place I thought of. I nestled myself in the circle window of his office. He would find me eventually.

It was snug in the little window. I could have fallen asleep, tucked away into the quiet corner, but my pant legs still clung to me with moisture. I closed my eyes and rested my head against the cool window glass. My eyes burned with emotion, and my cheeks flushed. Memories from earlier in the night surfaced again. No one was around to see my walls fall down. Lyla and I had been alone together so long, it has been strange to have someone regularly with us.

The house I was born in was well beyond repair. My parents had died a great many years ago. The little circle window in the cottage was between me and the harsh weather forming outside. My body was so overwhelmed with fatigue and sorrow.

There was a soft knock on the door. I didn't bother answering. Saxe would come in no matter what I did. "Cole?" He asked gently.

I felt him overlook me, so I said, "Up here, old man." Usually, that nickname brought about a giggle from Lyla and an eye roll from him. Now there was no humor in my voice, only a hollow echo of joy.

"Cole, why don't you come down? We'll make something to eat and discuss… business."

I was enraged. I jumped down from the window. "Business? Really? Is that all we ever were to you? What about us now? Will you keep us trapped here because I know all your secrets?"

"Cole, I-"

"Don't tell me you love her too! Did you raise her

from a toddler? Feed her for thirteen years? Where were you

all the other times I got beat up? What made you think you

could just snatch us from that life without any

repercussions?" I was yelling now. I had grown to love this

man. He had cared for me in a way no other adult ever had.

The sudden idea of prowling death had thrown the wool over

my eyes. I was lashing out at anyone near me, even myself.

"Please, listen to me, Cole. This is important. I

believe your-"

I was angry enough to actually try to hurt him. I

slashed my hand out, meaning to summon a spell of some

kind; instead, Lyla's walking stick flew into my hand.

I hit my knees. Any thought of anger melted away.

My eyes were glued to the staff. I was afraid of breaking it,

but I couldn't peel my fingers off of it. Saxe had helped Lyla

when I was powerless. This staff was a constant reminder of

how the playing field had shifted.

Saxe knelt beside me, "See Cole, even now I want to help you. All you have to do is let me."

I took a shuddering breath and nodded.

# Chapter Eleven:

# All Ides on Me

"It's early, and you are tired. Why don't you go to bed? We will talk more in the morning."

I nodded but doubted I would ever waste time sleeping, knowing that my days were numbered.

"And Cole?"

I lingered in the doorway of my bedroom. I did not turn around. I was ashamed of the fear that was evident on my face.

"Try not to dwell on the worst. There are still good things to come," Saxe promised.

I closed the door quietly behind me. I heard him pad past the door and begin the ascent up the stairs. I didn't want to risk waking Lyla, so I laid the walking stick next to her and just sat down on the floor next to my bed. It had a bad habit of squeaking, and I wanted to be alone. I brought my knees up and nestled my face between them. My throat constricted and fat, hot tears welled in me. I knew the noise from my crying would wake her up, but I didn't wish for Lyla's young eyes to watch me fall apart.

Before I could wake her, I jumped out the window and flew to the apple tree. Why did I find comfort in the branches of an apple tree that was decades older than I was? I sat in the fold of a branch, far enough from the ground that I couldn't be seen but too far in to see the stars. The air was warm, but the wind nipped at my exposed toes.

Death was coming. I could feel it wafting on the breeze and shaking the leaves from the trees. It whispered through the branches and up to meet me. I pulled my feet in, trying to keep the warmth that the sudden breeze was trying to steal. I put my head on my knees and closed my eyes.

I sat there until my back ached and my legs cramped. I slowly stretched out my legs and let life flow back into them. I straightened my neck and looked around. It wasn't a noise that alerted me; rather, the lack of it. The forest had gone completely silent.

A boy stood at the base of my tree. His face was still velveted in the shadows. How long had he been watching me? He made no move to attack or climb the tree after me. He just watched with his head slightly tilted as if he were evaluating me.

I jumped in fright and lost my balance. I tumbled from my limb but asked the wind to kindly not let me die. When I regained a good position, I searched for the boy, but he was gone. I flew around the base of the tree many times before finally spotting him at the top of a nearby hill. I touched gently down. The grass swayed beneath me as I took small steps forward. I looked up cautiously. Only an hour or so ago, the sky had been full of stars and planets alike. Now it was dark and cloudy. The only clear place was the moon. It was blood red.

Fear rooted me in place. He turned to look at me and I thought I saw his hand flick, beckoning me closer. I began walking up the hill. He stood frozen at the crest of the mountain. I pumped my legs faster.

When I was even with him, I could finally see his face. At least I would have been able to if he had one. Where his face should have been, a dark void floated. It was dark and frequently morphed as if he couldn't decide which face to use. A shiver ran up my spine. Finally, he settled back into his dark form without defined features. His fists clenched, and he launched himself at me. He barreled into me, and we fell backward. I tumbled into darkness.

I jumped awake and slipped off the fork in the tree where I had fallen asleep. I slammed into the limb beneath me and barely managed to grab on to it. My ribs ached, and my heart raced. It was just another dream.

I felt a moment of relief as I hauled myself into a crouch on the branch. Then I felt the fear rise up in me again. This development scared me even more. Was the future really this uncertain? Was the betrayal as set in stone as Saxe had made it seem? The sun had already begun rising, and the valley was flooded with golden light.

How could I stop myself from being tortured every night?

I stood up as an idea came to me. I got the visions as I slept. What if I could prevent that? Was it even possible? The hope of my plan filled me as surely as light filled the valley. I began descending.

I hated myself for considering it. Saxe had told me it was a burden. I tried to push away the nagging voice in the back of my mind that whispered my plan's flaws. I jumped down from the tree, and I raced into the cottage. Lyla was sitting at the kitchen island, sipping from a cup with curls of steam escaping from it. Saxe had his back to me. He busied himself with the kettle and dishes. He knew I was there, but he didn't want to speak with me. I didn't much want to either, but I had to.

"I had another vision," I said quietly.

His back straightened. "Already?"

I grimaced. "Yes."

"Do you know when it will happen?"

I closed my eyes and searched, "Um, not exactly."

"There were no defining features?"

I watched it replay in my mind again and again before recognizing the uniqueness of it. "The moon was red," I said finally. I opened my eyes to find him looking right at me. His eyes begged for forgiveness. He seemed to apologize for everything he couldn't control.

"A lunar eclipse," he breathed.

"What are we talking about?" Lyla whispered to me.

I waved her off. "Nothing."

She set her cup down loudly, some of the contents sloshing out. "No, I want to know. You both have been keeping secrets from me. I'm not just good at playing with flowers and being sweet. I can help you. Transparency, remember?"

Saxe and I looked at each other. I had forgotten about how fiery the young woman I had raised could be. "All right, Lyla. We're more involved in the prophecy than I realized. Four friends, dueling to the death. What should we do?"

"Kind of unlikely, don't you think? Cole doesn't have any friends."

I smiled smugly at him.

"Do we know when this will happen?" she asked.

"During a Lunar eclipse," Saxe provided, smiling proudly at her.

"Great, when's the next one?"

Saxe pulled a calendar from thin air. "April the tenth," he said. He pushed the calendar back into the air, and it disappeared.

"Great, so we have from today the…" she looked to Saxe for the date.

He pulled the calendar out again. "March the

fifteenth."

She nodded in thanks, and the calendar disappeared again. "March the fifteenth to April the tenth to prepare for this."

I smiled with Saxe, "I wish we'd included you sooner."

She shrugged and looked at the tea she had spilled. "I'm sorry, Mr. Saxe." She made the exact motions I had been practicing and made the tea float back into her cup.

I gaped at her.

She laughed. "You can't keep secrets from me, Cole. And I read a lot faster than you do."

I watched in awe as she picked up her tea cup and casually took a sip. She looked at me again. "What? What do you expect me to say?" She closed her eyes and moved her hands dramatically, "Ooh, Beware the Ides of March!" She chucked to herself and picked up her tea for another sip.

"Honestly…" she mumbled with an eye roll.

I pestered Saxe to start our preparations as soon as possible, but he insisted we have one last day of freedom before the hard stuff started. To honor that, Lyla and I spent the entire day outside. I suspected he only wanted us out so he could begin magical remedies or spells for our safety.

Darkness began to fall. My idea of avoiding sleep had festered and boiled inside me all day. I was confident I could do it. Then I would be free from the magic's deadly noose.

# Chapter Twelve:

## Sleepless in River Haven

What had started as a hope festered into an obsession. Sleeping scared me. My body would be completely shut off, at the utter mercy of whatever magic possessed me. I was tortured by the sight of the same dream over and over, constantly replaying in my mind.

So I stopped sleeping.

The first night was easy. I got plenty of stuff done. I cleaned up the bedroom until Lyla hissed, "Can it, Cole!" I practiced all of my magic, not just air. I picked up the kitchen and started warming the stove for breakfast. When I heard Saxe getting ready upstairs, I hurried to the bedroom.

I wasn't doing anything wrong, but I knew he wouldn't like it, so I hid when he came down the stairs. Day one, and I pulled it off.

Day two was nearly as easy as the first. Why hadn't I done this weeks ago? I glanced around our bedroom. Tidy and clean. I quietly opened the door and slipped into the kitchen. Everything was in its place. I had done my job too well the night before. I slipped out the front door and into the night air. A cool breeze nipped at my heels as if begging me to take it on an adventure.

I flew over the cottage and into the woods with a little help from the wind. I brushed past treetops and around mountains and flew over ponds and rivers. I only stopped in the wake of an oak tree the size of a house. I looped around it a couple times before a flit of music drifted to my ears.

"Did you hear that?" I asked the breeze. I whirled around, trying to find the source. I pointed over the treetops to a distant glow. "There!" I dashed over the rest of the land before crashing into the tree line not far from the small village.

I emerged from the forest, brushing leaves and mud from my sleeves. No one noticed the stranger that had just fallen from the sky. People danced in complicated circles as they sang around the fire, keeping up with the merriment as if had always been there. I could not catch the words to their song, but they came fast. The dancer's feet created a complicated rhythm that the words marched to. The distraction gave me a chance to explore and ask around.

"Do you know a Saxe, by any chance?"

The old man grinned. "Yeah, I know him!" His accent was heavily foreign.

"You do?"

"O'course! He came by not too long ago."

"Really? What do you know about him?"

"Oh, he's quite the queer fellow. Always talking to his goat. But always very open."

"He travels with a goat?"

"And you don't?" The man laughed and went back to his drinking.

I asked the lady behind the counter if she knew Saxe.

She threw her towel over her shoulder with a glare. "If I remembered the name of every man I ever served, I wouldn't have room for anything else."

I turned to the man who had just come to sit on the stool next to me. "Do you know Mark Saxe?"

"Scram off," he muttered and grabbed a glass of whatever the lady was serving.

I sheepishly walked away from the bar. A little boy ran up to me. He flashed a huge grin and asked me if I would like to play Bimsy with him. I nodded with a smile.

Bimsy was a dangerous game and not for the faint of heart. You needed at least two players and a wide, open area without many people around. The goal of the game was to hit your opponent with a rock, the catch was that you could only use your feet. You could play the rock off of anything it bounced off of, including passersby. The game was famous among children and infamous among adults. Children always walked away bloodied or bruised. It was a good time, if you had the right partner.

As we kicked the rock he'd chosen, I began grilling him with questions. "Have you always lived here?"

"Yessir."

"Are there any more towns nearby?"

"No, sir, just in Rolling Acres."

I looked over at the weather-worn traveler I had

spoken to moments earlier. He squinted at me as suspicion squirmed in my gut. "Does anyone live down by the Calfkiller River?" I kicked the rock over the fire and back towards him.

The rock skidded to a stop at his feet. He did not bend down to pick it up or kick it back to me. His eyes were startlingly focused on me. From my side of the bonfire, he appeared to be calmly standing in the middle of the blaze. The flames seemed to eat him alive without scorching him. His eyes glowed like embers. "Odd things happen down there. Livestock that wanders down there never return. People vanish into thin air, only to return a few days later. So to answer your question, sir, no. Nobody with a heart still beating lives down there. We call that place Deadwood."

"No one has ever come back from Deadwood?"

"People do, but they don't remember what they saw

or how they got back to town. Animals never come back."

"I see."

He kicked the rock, and it soared straight through the fire and into me. I grunted, and he cheered.

"Rematch?" he asked hopefully.

I smiled and looked up at the moon. It was time to start heading back. "No, I'm afraid I have to go."

"Where?"

"Deadwood."

The look on his face was one of absolute horror. I gave him a grin and threw the rock back at him. He caught it and silently watched me disappear back into the trees.

River Haven was only an hour from there as the Cole flies. Saxe was preparing breakfast when I arrived. I snuck in through the window and sat in bed until Lyla began to stir. Night two was a win.

As day three wore on, my weariness began to mount. As the sun went down, the drowsiness slammed into me. I felt haunted. Everything the little boy had said about the Deadwood echoed around me. The darkness reflected even the slightest of sounds, so I wandered back outside. I practiced all of the elements before growing tired of the repetition. I could feel myself teetering on the edge of sleep.

I barely managed to fly myself back to the town. I was surprised to find the tiny village still active. People danced around the fire, men drank themselves to sleep. The young boy I had talked to previously stood alone, watching the circles of people dance.

I walked up beside him. He didn't acknowledge me except for a slight nod. We stood in reverent silence, watching the rows upon rows of dancers.

The inner-circle consisted of the most talented

dancers. They spun and moved in rhythm with the fire's dance with ease. The outer ring was primarily children or older folks who couldn't dance as well. The inner circle consisted of intermediate dancers who knew most of the dance but were not masters.

The words of their song echoed back from the mountains and washed over me like a waterfall.

"When shall come the boy, who carries wounds and woe?" the inner circle sang. The middle ring answered, "He shall bring the questions." Finally, the children shouted back, "Oh me, oh my. Please, more!"

The little boy broke the spell the singing had created. "You're back," he said quietly.

"Why aren't you dancing?"

"Can't."

"Can't or won't?"

He shrugged and turned to look at me. "Are you dead?"

I patted myself with a grin. "I don't think so."

He faced the dancers. The second verse of the song was starting. It was formatted like the first, with the music originating from the center and echoing from the rings.

"When shall come the heir to a lying throne? He shall save him with his words. Oh me, oh my. Please more!"

"Then you lied," the boy stated plainly.

"About what?"

"No one comes back from Deadwood."

"I did."

The villagers were singing again. "When shall come the royal, tough as diamond coal? She befriends him when she comes. Oh me, oh my. Please more!"

He looked up at me. "Who are you?" His eyes were

not the eyes of a boy but the eyes of a wise old man. He acted with the knowledge of an experienced man, not a child.

My heart pounded. Did I say my real name? Would he tell anyone about me? "Er... Jack," I said. "You are?"

"Will." He shook my hand.

The song was reaching its crescendo. "When shall come the orphan, desperate, lone, and hurt? He brings darkness as he comes. Oh me, oh my." Instead of the children's plea for more, the entire village joined in. Men at the bar, young women corralling children, and old women from back porches. They each yodeled out an "oh me, oh my," before the dancing rings began harmonizing in the very last "Oh-oh!" The onlookers cheered, and the dancers dispersed. Some of the singers went to the bar, some ran to the waiting arms of the families. Still, others just disappeared into the night.

"What was all that?" I asked, gesturing to everyone around us.

"They're celebrating Full Spring."

"And that's an all-night event?"

He nodded. "Four nights in a row."

He took me to an empty table and sat down, his eyes never leaving the dancing people.

I nodded as well. "Looks like fun."

"To most. Not to me."

"Will," I began, "do you know a man by the name of Saxe?"

He shook his head. "I don't, and neither does anyone else here."

"But they all say they did."

"And they each gave a different description, didn't they?"

I nodded slowly.

"He's nothing but trouble, Jack. If you really insist on speaking with him, I'll take you."

"In Deadwood?"

"No, he's been at the inn for a few weeks now."

My head spun. "Did he mention his first name?"

Will shook his head.

I stood up quickly. If it wasn't Mark Saxe, it had to be the evil brother Saxe. Saxe's words echoed in my brain. *My brother resented me for it.* He had said. *He considered killing me because I had no heir.* "I've got to get out of here," I turned and began pacing for the trees.

"Wait!" Will cried.

I turned in the tree line, my heart beating wildly.

"Beating death once is a feat already. But twice into Deadwood?" He paused and studied me. He seemed to see

227

right through my tired and disheveled appearance. "That's suicide."

I smiled at his kindness. "I'll be alright."

The fear in his eyes didn't waver.

I ran into the trees. The more I pumped my legs, the better I felt. I didn't feel as tired as the cool night air swept over me. I only paused when I zipped through the tree line and into sight of the cottage.

I stopped to catch my breath. The exhaustion was maddening. I could feel myself losing my grip.

I was mostly unaware of how tired I was when I was active. To fight the fatigue, I put myself through rigorous exercise. The motion kept me sharp, but the instant I stopped, the weariness tripled. I ran the field's length, swam upstream, and climbed the tree.

At the dawn of the fourth day, I barely dragged

myself inside in time to stand inside the bedroom. I knew if I laid down on the bed or on the floor, I would strain to get up again. I drug myself through the day, barely managing to function.

Night four of no sleep was deadly. My body was dead weight, and refused to let any magic flow through me. Without the practice, the night passed painfully slowly. Part of me wanted to go see Will. But the other part of me knew the threat Saxe's brother posed. If he managed to catch me now, I would have no way to defend myself. No magic and no energy to fight.

Instead, I walked up and down the river bed. The cold water kept me from falling over. I knew if I stopped moving, I would never begin again.

Giant fish dwelled nearby, lurking in the shadows, waiting to devour me. One lunged at me, and I stumbled from the water. From then on, I walked beside the water, not in it.

My eyes drooped, and I kept stumbling. A bear appeared on the other side of the river. A fish grew legs and chased me around the yard. The cottage seemed slanted and wrong.

I closed my eyes and fell to my knees. I covered my ears against the roar of static. I crawled to the edge of the water and tried to avoid the giant fish with large eyes. I splashed my face.

My stomach lurched as the cold hit me. I slung my hair from my eyes and stood up.

The fish was gone. The cabin was back to normal again. River Haven was its usual, peaceful self.

I heaved myself down, realizing the vastness of my problems. I didn't know what was real anymore. Was the stream really moving that fast, or was my brain just too slow to comprehend? Was the apple tree bending menacingly over me, or was that the wind?

I didn't realize it, but I had sunk back onto the damp grass. I clutched the grass, trying to get a grip on what was really happening. The stream gurgled, and the wind blew. I could hear someone walking towards me. I ripped up the grass and threw it at whoever was coming my way.

I sat up and looked around, expecting an evil Saxe twin. Only the wind moved. Not a soul was in sight. "Fine!" I yelled. Then I remembered that Saxe and Lyla were sleeping inside and dropped my voice to a whisper. "Fine, you win!" I closed my eyes, releasing myself to the mercy of my exhaustion. I felt myself melting into the grass.

I was relaxed.

I was calm.

I wasn't asleep.

So I laid there longer. The grass was soft, and the dirt smelled rich. I stared up at the ever-changing night sky. I let my mind wander. I closed my eyes and listened to the rustle of the stream.

I never drifted off. When I opened my eyes again, the sky was beginning to lighten.

Why couldn't my body just shut off?

I was still terrified of whatever magic had its hooks in me. I still didn't want to surrender to that.

I barely managed to open my eyes again. I wanted to float leisurely to the window, but I couldn't muster any magic. I stood up and pulled myself to the door, not caring that Saxe was standing nearby. He watched me with concern as I drug my feet into the bedroom. I struggled through the door and collapsed onto the bed. My arms felt heavy, and my toes required too much energy to move. I closed my eyes, trying to welcome the darkness. The instant my eyes closed, that formless face floated lunged at me from the void. My eyes wouldn't stay closed for long.

The sun rose and dragged me into another day.

Day five. I had gone weeks without food and shelter. But could barely last five days without sleep?

When Lyla got up, so did I.

I trudged into the kitchen, not even caring to pretend I wasn't tired.

I sat heavily at the kitchen island and took the chance to bang my head into the stone a few times.

Saxe put a hand on my shoulder. I dropped my shoulders into a slump and let out a groan of frustration. "Stop this. I know what you've been doing the past few nights. I'm sorry this happened to you, but you will only be more miserable," he said.

"I learned that lesson the hard way. I-I can't sleep."

"Are you sure you tried?"

I lifted my head to look him in the eyes. "I will lay in bed all night, unmoving, just staring at your beautiful ceiling, to prove it if you want."

"We'll eat, and you can go take a nap."

"Yes, please."

I propped my elbow on the table and rested my chin on my hand. I muscled through the eggs and toast. Saxe and Lyla tried to engage me in conversation, but my mind couldn't stay focused long enough to listen.

"Mr. Saxe, please, just let him go to bed," Lyla said after repeating herself for the fourth time.

"Go on, Cole. I'll wake you for lunch."

I sighed.

"If I let you sleep any later, you won't sleep

tonight."

I doubted it would make a difference.

I stumbled into the bedroom and closed the windows and doors. It was dark enough, so I rolled myself in a sheet and closed my eyes.

I wonder if Saxe has met any other magical creatures. Like dragons. Or elves.

I rolled over.

Go.

To.

Sleep.

What if I held my breath until I passed out? Would that help me?

I covered my face with my pillow.

Sleep.

I laid there, trying to count sheep or clouds or

whatever it is people tell you. It wasn't long before I heard

Saxe knock on my door. Light streamed into the door, and I

rolled over to avoid the excess light.

"No luck?"

"None whatsoever."

I stood up, fighting off the dizziness that

accompanied it. I leaned on the doorway for support. How

could I be this tired and not be able to sleep?

"This is ridiculous." Saxe walked in front of me. He

grabbed my arm.

I kept my eyes downcast, trying to save energy

where I could. "I can't very well help it! I've done everything

I can!" He gripped my arm tighter. "Let go of me."

I tried to pull away from him.

Lyla stepped forward. "Cole, maybe you should just-

"

"No!" I pulled against Saxe again. I turned around to look at Lyla. "I don't want to listen to anyone else tell me what I should or shouldn't do! You don't know what I've gone through! You don't understand what's happening to me!"

Saxe pulled me around again. "Stop! Just let go!" I finally looked up to meet his gaze. The instant our eyes locked, my knees buckled. I sank into his shoulder, I tried to grab onto his shirt, but my fingers shook. All of my weight crashed into him. His strong arms caught me and tried to pull me upright again. I distantly heard Lyla scream my name. I couldn't keep my eyes open long enough to apologize. I sank into the long-dreaded void of darkness that awaited me.

. . .

I saw every vision I'd ever had float by me a dozen times. They all mixed until a mangled version of it haunted me. I wanted to wake up, end this, but something pushed me back down every time I tried.

It must be magic. Saxe had used something already in my mind against me. His magic pulsed and breathed as I did, but I was trapped under his spell.

. . .

My eyes snapped open. I felt Saxe's magic flee out of me. I sat up, but a wave of dizziness overtook me. Where was I?

I flung my feet off the bed and tried to stand up. My feet were numb and unresponsive. My knees buckled and wouldn't bear the weight of my body. I fell back onto the bed.

It yelped loudly under the sudden weight. The door squeaked open, light flooded the room. I gasped and covered my eyes.

"How do you feel?" a voice said.

"Blind."

The door closed, and someone shuffled forward. My eyes adjusted again to see an old man. He looked as tired as I was. He knelt in front of me and put a hand on my knee.

"You scared Lyla to death."

The memory of everything I'd done came rushing forward and flooded my mind. Another wave of mental exhaustion hit me, and I swayed. Saxe put a hand on my shoulder to steady me.

"Why did you lie to us?"

"I..." my voice faltered. I bit my lip as shame heated my cheeks. "I'm terrified," I confessed. As I spoke, Saxe rose to sit next to me. "I don't know what's coming. I don't have any control over what's going to happen. All I see, night after night, is the one person I would give my life to protect… die right in front of me. There's nothing I can do to stop it. I see it over and over. It's burnt into my memory."

I took a deep breath before continuing. "I wanted to stop it. All of it. So I didn't let myself have the chance to see it again. I pushed myself past my limits. I… I just want it to *stop*."

"I understand. I did something similar in my youth. The side effects were much more… permanent, though."

For the first time, I noticed the scars on his wrists. His usually long sleeve had shifted up to reveal a nasty scar that spread up his arm.

"How are you really feeling?"

"Awful." My words seemed slurred. "I can barely keep my eyes open."

I noticed I had been leaning on him for support.

"Good. Then it worked."

"Worked? What worked?" I said, nodding off momentarily.

"The parasite." He stood up, and my only support went with him.

I sat up quickly, trying to compensate for nearly falling over. "Parasite? You gave me a parasite?"

"Yes, to drain you of any remaining energy."

"What?"

"It takes a very strong-willed magician to fight one of those off, and in under two hours. I'm impressed. Especially while unconscious. In all honesty, I'm surprised you're awake right now."

I smiled weakly. "Am I, though?"

"Now you're left with real fatigue. You should sleep

soundly for a while."

"But a parasite? Was that really necessary?"

He nodded. "To show you just how strong you are. Goodnight, Cole. And thank you."

"Thank me? For what?"

I could practically hear the slight smile on his face. "Transparency."

He turned on his heel and left. Lyla's voice echoed in my mind. She must have come forward with our conversation. An odd image popped into my brain. The two of them sitting alone, each taking turns pouring out my secrets. I didn't have the strength to feel betrayed. I laid back down and rolled over.

It was the best night's sleep I'd had in years.

# Chapter Thirteen:

# Doomsday Prepping

The side effects of the parasite did not stay with me for very long. Neither did Saxe's sympathy for me. The following day, he put me to work. I was still tired but not as exhausted as I had been only a day before. Now that I could function properly, I could see my folly. Although I had somewhat good intentions, there was no way I could have kept it up.

I still lay awake at night, fearful of myself. What if it happened again? What if I couldn't sleep? Why had my brain locked down when I needed it to shut off? Every part of my mind screamed that I would never sleep regularly again. Yet every morning, I awoke, unsure of when I slept or how.

Lyla was hurt by my words, but even more so by my

actions. She was curt with me for several days before I finally got up the guts to apologize. She had nodded but had not said anything. I could tell she was still hurt, but I didn't know how to fix it. I remembered how much fun it had been gliding around the pond. I found an old picnic table a few feet into the tree line. I lifted on one side and asked the wind to lift the other. I carried it into the water's edge.

I took a deep breath and hoped it worked. I got behind it and pushed. I asked the wind to pick up on the nose of the old table, praying it wouldn't fall apart. Soon after, I was zooming around the river on a picnic table. When I was sure I could hold both of our weights, I parked it on the river bank.

I knocked on our door, and it swung inward. "Lyla?"

"Hmm?" She didn't look up from her book.

Actually, *my* book. The self-written book on magic from

Saxe.

"Could you come outside?"

"I understand; you're sorry. Now can I finish my chapter?"

"It won't take long," I begged.

She finally set her book down and looked at me. She got up and followed me out the door.

"Would you sit at the picnic table?"

She paused on the rocky shore as I waded into the ankle-deep water.

"I don't think it'll hold me," she said hesitantly, drawing back.

I jumped up onto the table. I heard a quiet crack as it buckled under my weight. I covered my uncertainty with a wild grin. "It will, I promise." I squatted down and offered her a hand.

She weighed my word against the rickety, rotten, unstable picnic table I was kneeling on. Nature had not been kind to the old wood boards. The weather had beaten against the sides and moss patches created a mismatched quilt across the top. She took a deep breath and kicked off her shoes. She splashed through the water and sat down on the bench connected to the table.

I smiled. "Okay, now hang on tight."

"What?"

I began pushing on the back of the table. The wind picked up the front, and we were off. I swung myself up and stood on the top of the table. To steer, all I had to do was lean. The wind on my face and the sun on my back felt amazing. I spread out my arms and closed my eyes, and felt like I was flying across the water.

I let out a joyful yell and listened to it echo across

the surface of the river. Lyla did the same. I opened my eyes and looked down at her. Her grin was nearly as big as mine. She extended her hand to me, so I clasped it and helped her up. I stayed on the back of our makeshift boat while she hobbled to the front. She knelt down and looked underneath as if I had strapped the table to a giant fish. She reached down and put her hand in the water. She accidentally sprayed herself and rocked back on her heels to wipe her face.

She looked at me with a sympathetic smile. I smiled back at her. I tried to convey just how sorry I was. I was sorry for snapping. I was sorry for letting this happen to us. I was sorry I couldn't protect her like I should. I was sorry for not being transparent enough with her.

I looked ahead of us and saw a small island made of rocky soil that stuck out of the water only a few inches. I leaned as far as I could to the left just as she sat up. She tumbled to the right and off the table boat. I heard a huge splash and a strangled, "Cole!" I grimaced and pulled back to circle around. When I pulled up beside her, she was soaked but still laughing.

"Help me up," she said with a smile. This time we both sat at the back of the table. She had her back to the water while I had my back to River Haven.

"So a table boat?"

"Yeah, one of my better schemes."

She shrugged. "One of your better-executed schemes."

"Touché."

"But you didn't just bring me out here to show off, did you?"

"No."

"Go ahead."

"Lyla, I'm sorry. I really didn't mean to say all of that. I was delirious and not thinking straight and-"

"That's what delirious means."

"Well, maybe I still am."

She laughed.

"But the heart of the matter is: I'm not mad at you. I never was. I'm mad at myself and my own incompetence."

"Transparency, thank you."

"Still working on it."

"I'm sorry I didn't try harder to help you."

"There's nothing you can do."

"That doesn't mean I can't try."

I gave her a smile. Honesty tugged at my heartstrings again. Should I tell her what I see every night? I should let her know what's coming. I opened my mouth as she giggled and rung out her shirt over the side. I closed my mouth again and flashed a fake smile.

"I have a question," she said, leaning back on her hands. "Does this vision you get every night block all others?"

I dangled one of my feet over the side and into the water. "Other what?" I asked.

"Other glimpses of the future."

"Oh, I don't really get any other ones."

"Maybe you can. What if you could see into any little pocket of the future?"

"That would be fun," I guessed, splashing her playfully.

"Maybe the one at night is blocking them from coming. Maybe it's like a switch; you just have to flip it on during the day."

I began steering us back towards River Haven. "Or

maybe you are too positive."

She laughed, and I blasted us into full speed.

Saxe was waiting for us when I pulled onto the shore. "You've progressed nicely," he commented when I parked the table on the beach.

"Anything... new?"

I knew what he meant. Lyla looked at me fearfully. I looked back at her, trying to pretend I didn't know what he meant. "No," I said.

. . .

Every morning he pestered me about every detail. The day, the time, the place, people present, types of magic. Every scrap of information he could peel out of me. But every vision was the same. They all happened in the same place, time, and the same people were there. How long could I withstand his pressuring?

The days passed slowly. Saxe watched me like a hawk. I had lost his trust, and rightfully so. The only thing that made the day bearable was Lyla. She had forgiven me and gave me a new idea. I hadn't yet been able to see anything other than my normal vision, but I was nearly there. Sometimes I could see doubles of something slightly out of place. I pointed this out to her one morning. She slapped me on the back and congratulated me for being a drunk. We often practiced together, or, better yet, we practiced on each other.

We stood on the front lawn. I closed my eyes, trying to block out the dream I had seen again last night. I tried to picture the wind sweeping the valley like a giant eagle or some other proud creature.

The grass swayed in a gentle wind beneath me. I

took that wind and thrust it outwards. I could feel it sweeping across the valley and brushing up the apple tree. I flirted with the river and splashed Lyla. I opened my eyes and laughed at her.

She had been ankle-deep in the cold waters, redirecting the current for her shell collection. She had rolled up the ends of her trousers to keep them dry, but thanks to me the bottom half of her pants were splattered wet spots. Saxe had offered her a dress, but she had chosen the pants. He had given me new clothes as well. It had been strange not wearing the same clothes every day. I got to change shirts or pants whenever I wanted. I rarely did, but it was nice to have fresh shirts at my disposal.

Lyla grinned mischievously at me. She took her walking stick out from under her arm and twirled it over the water. She allowed the water to rise and float over to me. I waited until the last possible second, then let the wind zip me away. The water splashed onto the empty ground.

Lyla turned to watch me fly. I dipped my hand into the water and made it splash her in the face. I touched down in the shallow water where the reeds grew. She made a face at me. I crossed my arms and stuck out my tongue. She made the water cover my feet and sucked me into the river.

I landed with a resounding splash; in turn, it also splashed her. I pulled the pebbles she was standing on out from under her. She landed next to me in a bundle of laughter and water droplets. Her shirt and pants were soaked, and most of her pebbles and shells had spilled from her pockets. Her hair dangled in front of her face like a curtain. She separated it and slung it back over her head, slinging a twirl of water that came raining back down on us.

I stood up and shook out my hair on her. She

laughed and kicked water at me. "You better be careful, little lady," I said as I wrung out my shirt, "you never know when I might…" when I looked back, she was gone. "Lyla? Ha, very clever." I turned in a full circle but couldn't see her. "How are you doing this? Did you turn into a fish? Why didn't I learn that one?"

But when I looked back to land, the sky darkened. The sun morphed into a blood-red moon. I stumbled as I tried to get out of the river. I saw the shadowy figure who had come to haunt my nightmares at the top of the hill. He had his back to me. I hoped I could sneak up on him, but then he turned to face me. He smiled, then dissolved into smoke. Moments later, an army charged over the hill. I stumbled back. There were at least a hundred men, and they all resembled the thugs that had attacked us in the alleyway. They saw me and howled a battle cry. They ran towards me, and I stumbled. I tripped and fell into the water.

I opened my eyes to find Lyla beside me again. "I don't remember you being so clumsy," she said, laughing.

"You mean… you didn't see any of that?"

Her smile fell. "Any of what?"

My heart raced. "I was wrong before. The Four won't meet in a month."

"What do you mean?"

"There's an army coming, Lyla. At least a hundred fully grown men, like the ones who attacked us before."

She shuddered, and it wasn't because of the frigid waters running under us.

I jumped up and helped her rise. "Come on, we've got to get started."

"On what?"

"Doomsday preparations." Why had Saxe waited

this long to start them anyway?

We ran to the cottage door and barged inside.

"Saxe!" I called.

"Mr. Saxe?" Lyla echoed.

No one answered. "Try his study," I explained as I raced up the stairs.

"Saxe?" I called.

His door was open just a crack. "We have news about the-" I moved to knock on the door, and it swung inward. "Saxe!" I barreled through the doorway and to his side. Lyla caught the swinging door and stifled a gasp. He was lying on the floor, clutching his abdomen. "What happened?"

"It's getting worse," he whispered. He tried to get up, but a new wave of pain crashed over him.

I slung his arm over my shoulder to help him up.

Lyla did the same on his other side. "I think I know why."

His eyebrows went up as I helped him into a chair.

"River Haven is going to be attacked, and we haven't even started preparing. Tenth of April, remember?"

"My brother," he growled. "We haven't a moment to lose." He tried to stand up, but his face contorted with pain.

"Also, I think I know where he's hiding."

He kept his arms hugging his sides and tried to sit up. "The village just North of here?" He gasped and laid back down.

"Yes, how did you know?"

He grimaced as he sat up again. "Just call it intuition."

I gave him my hand and helped him into his chair.

"Is there anything we can do to help you?" Lyla asked from behind me.

He smiled weakly. "I am afraid not, my dear. We can only wait for it to pass."

She inched past me to sit at his feet. "Why would someone do this to you?" she asked, putting her hand on his knee."

"He has always detested me. Jealousy does terrible things to people's minds."

"I'm sorry," she said quietly.

He smiled at her, "There's nothing you could do to help, child, but I appreciate the sentiment."

I stood back and watched her weave her magic. With love and understanding, she healed him. Her smile could close the deepest wound and thaw the coldest heart. She chatted with him, and as the conversation progressed, his groans grew fewer and fewer until he patted her hand thankfully and rose.

"Thank you very much, dear, now where should we start?"

. . .

We could have started by letting the disgruntled Pixie out to anger our attackers. We could have built a magical wall around the perimeter of River Haven. But we didn't. We started with the garden. Because harvesting magical herbs and food of all kinds is precisely how I'd protect my house.

"Shouldn't we do this last?" Lyla voiced while plucking cherry tomatoes for the vine.

I struggled to pull up a carrot that was wedged into the ground. I was afraid if I pulled too hard, the center of the earth might come up with it.

"Won't this all spoil before the month is over?" she asked. She held the hem of her overly large shirt close to her body to create a pocket to fill with her harvest. Her pyramid was overflowing with tiny, juicy berries.

I envied the fruits of her labor. She had dozens of tomatoes while I had a measly three carrots.

Saxe chuckled. "One thing I've learned in my years is that time is never kind. We think we have a few weeks, but time may play a nasty trick and move around on us. Suddenly the date is upon us, and we have no food and nothing done."

"Oh," Lyla breathed.

I gave one final yank on the carrot that was giving me fits. It came loose, and my hands sprung free. I landed on my rump with clods of dirt raining down on me.

Saxe chuckled while Lyla busted out laughing. Her sides shook violently. She dropped the front of her shirt, and the tomatoes scattered out from her makeshift apron. I picked up a couple while dusting off my shirt.

"Thanks. I'll be here all week to keep you entertained."

Saxe chuckled and began helping Lyla retrieve her tomatoes. "We're going to need your antics. I intend for us to remain inside for most of the coming weeks."

I dropped my carrot. "What? What will we do? Stare at each other awkwardly?" I froze and dropped my gaze. We had that down to a science already.

"We will find something to do. We may not enjoy all of it, but it is better than the alternative."

"Which is?"

"Being outside during the battle. I am growing weaker by the day. It will be easier for me to defend only the cottage rather than the entirety of River Haven."

I wanted to press for more time, but I saw the worry in his eyes. Worse still, I saw the lines in his face and the bags under his eyes that hadn't been there a few days ago. He was fading fast, and he wanted to keep us safe. All he asked of me was to stay inside for a few days.

I nodded, "Alright, but what else can we do to help?"

He stood up shakily. "Go inside the kitchen and find the big clay jar in one of my tall cabinets."

I ran inside and looked at his vast array of cabinets. I climbed onto the counter and searched the one above the cold box. There was nothing but spare cutlery. Each cabinet held new surprises and more stuff, but none had a large clay jar. Lyla wobbled in and laughed at the sight of me. I did look ridiculous. I was standing with one foot on the counter, stretching as far as I could, with my head and arms in a cabinet poking around.

I asked the air to assist her as she climbed up with me. She chuckled as she opened a cabinet at my chest height and pulled out a jar that matched Saxe's description.

I helped her jump down. "How did you know that?"

She tucked her staff under one arm and punched me playfully in the arm. "Woman's intuition."

She handed Saxe the jar, and we watched with excited anticipation. When he opened the lip, I expected a magical whoosh or a spell to spill through the seal. Instead, when he opened the lid, there was just the regular pop from the seal. He took out a pinch and ground it between his fingers. We watched the flaky white stuff fall back into the jar.

"Is that… salt?" Lyla asked. I could tell she was trying to mask her disappointment.

"Yes, I harvested it from the Narrows myself. Took hours to cure and many trips to acquire the whole jar, but today will make it worth the effort."

"What will *salt* do against an army?" Lyla asked.

I pretended to hold a fistful of the powdery stuff. I dodged imaginary hits and threw the useless powder at my pretend adversary. "Yes! I temporarily blinded him! Now we just have to find a way to defend the rest of the cottage since I'm out of salt!"

"Believe it or not, salt is good for more than flavoring food." Saxe handed us each a handful. "Line the windows, and I'll line the doorways."

I did as I was told with fleeting reassurance that he wasn't going looney. If this actually protected us against coming evils, I wanted Lyla's bedroom to be the safest one. I applied a thick line on the windowsill between our beds, whispering a prayer that it would be enough. I climbed the stairs and entered the study. There was a length of long windows on the wall behind his desk. I sprinkled a line at the base of those windows, then floated up to line the circular window above them. It was cracked open slightly to allow a breeze to swirl in.

As I flew back to the door, I noticed something shift in the wind that followed me. I flew back and touched down in front of the fireplace.

I sifted through the warm ashes and found bits of paper. The writing looked familiar. I blew the ash from it and held it up to the light. The title read *The Foreseen Four*. A pang of recognition hit me. These were the notes I had stolen from him all those months ago.

Most of it was burned beyond recognition, but there were remains of a leather string wrapping around it. Why had

Saxe burned this? Well, he tried to burn it. Was this why his brother was attacking River Haven? If so, how would he explain us? The prophecy never differentiated male or female, so for all I knew, Lyla was just as much a part of this as I was. Now all he needed was the other two. Saxe was halfway to changing the world. If he was so quick to burn the only physical evidence, what else was he planning?

"Are you temporarily blinded?" Lyla called from the base of the steps.

I jumped and threw the papers back in the fireplace and shook the ash from my hands. "Yes, a ton of windows up here."

"Don't forget the bedroom!"

I paused in the study's doorway. I didn't really want to go into Saxe's bedroom. That felt invasive and private. Then I remembered I had just dug through the ashtray of his fireplace.

The upstairs only had two rooms off the landing: the study and Saxe's bedroom. Apparently, he spent the bulk of his time next door. A single square window, a bed, a dresser with a notebook on top, and a closet that held a few shirts, pants, and a single traveling cloak.

I laid a salt line across the window sill and walked back out the door.

# Chapter Fourteen:

# Beginning of the End

We locked and bolted all the doors, even though no one was in sight. It felt strange to deadlock all the doors but still sleep with a window open.

My entire life has been go, go, go. Run, new town, run, new town. Steal this, escape from that. I had never known boredom.

This was going to kill me.

Day one: I read the book Saxe had given me. I'd finished all the basics, and was now learning about incantations, verbal and nonverbal spells, triggers, placement charms, and, believe it or not, the many properties of salt.

I had re-read the ominous ending chapter. But there was nothing past the initial warning. Only blank pages. Was

Saxe planning on writing more? Should I ask him about it? Should I pretend to not notice?

I acted like reading was difficult, which it was, and that I was reading in order, which I wasn't. Lyla was keen on reading but insisted I also instruct her. The first few times were disastrous. But I began to notice my own skills increasing as we worked together.

Day two: hiding under the kitchen island and practicing my diversion spells to keep from talking to anyone. I am increasingly terrible at avoiding people.

Day three... I am now considering crawling out of the window.

I love Lyla to death, but I can't be doing something with her all hours of the day. We have made muffins, pumpkin bread, and invented something she calls 'Gamoots'. A small piece of dough surrounds a magical gooey substance but disappears after heat is applied. We've also concocted a strange drink that keeps bubbles and burns my nose.

After trying every combination in Saxe's kitchen, he suggested we try playing a game. We played tag, but it didn't last long. After well over a hundred rounds of hide and seek, we had exhausted every nook and cranny of the cottage. The only rooms upstairs were Saxe's bedroom and the study, but neither of us wanted to hide in there. The downstairs consisted of the kitchen, the bedroom, a bathroom, and a sunroom. Saxe would play with us every so often, but he spent most of his time in his study.

He was terrific at helping us with our magical learning, which we practiced for hours every day. He was surprisingly an excellent teacher beyond his expertise. Under his guidance, Lyla and I learned to write. A necessary skill I never required before now. We began advanced reading. Lyla especially enjoyed these when applied together. She had a higher capacity for learning than I ever would.

When we were forced to build on our creative writing, I would stare at a tree for a while and try to find an adjective to describe it that wasn't 'green' or 'tall'. Lyla flourished when I struggled. Her eloquent words filled the page with rhythm, rhyme, and iambic pentameter. While I was preoccupied with the little stream of words I wrote, she constructed a fountain of words for everyone to see in wonder and amazement.

I am sad to say I was slightly jealous. I could see the pride in Saxe's eyes when he read her work. I saw nothing but grammar mistakes when he read mine. I stuck to what I had an unnatural knack for: magic.

We practiced daily, but each day was new. Sometimes we did drills; other times, we did interactive activities. My favorite was the trust exercises. When Lyla was utterly at my mercy, or when I was at hers. It reminded me of the days when that was true. There was a time when we really were all the other had. We had to lean on each other because the world had turned its back on us.

Now, we had magic, and we could read, write, add, subtract, and multiply. Was this what it felt like to be growing apart? I still loved her, but I saw less and less of the child I knew and more and more of the woman she was becoming.

. . .

I jumped awake after seeing the same dream again. It was stifling in the little room. The door was closed, and the window didn't provide the usual breeze.

I was stir crazy. Another week of this would kill me long before a thug had the chance. I longed absentmindedly for action. Really, anything that wasn't this. I would have danced around a fire for full spring. I would have played Bimsy with Will. Even taking a walk outside would do. I watched a bluejay flit through the air and sing to whoever was listening at this early hour.

I wanted to climb out the window and be free like a small bird. I was almost out when a tingle of recognition seized me. I had read something about a situation like mine. It was easy to get out but much harder to get in. The salt guarded the house no matter who was trying to get inside. It didn't discriminate between a murderer, a burglar, or the homeowner.

I looked at the sleeping form of Lyla, then back at my chance to escape for just a few hours. I climbed back down out of the window and sat down on the edge of my bed. I didn't want to leave Lyla stranded here while I was outside.

I still was not tired, so I eased the door open and walked into the kitchen. I intended to sit in the sunroom and look at the stars or open the front door just to sit behind the salt, imagining freedom. Instead, I sat down on a stool by the island. Saxe was seated next to me.

"Couldn't sleep?" I asked.

He shook his head.

I knew the feeling. I paused, wanting to continue but doubting if it was wise. I turned to look at his silhouette in the moonlight. "Can I ask you something?"

He blinked hard and looked at me. "Anything."

I took a deep breath. "Why did you burn those papers?"

A small smile stretched across his face. "You saw

that, did you?"

I nodded.

He smiled and turned to face me. "I think there is more going on than meets the eye. Isn't it strange how he decided to attack when I found one of the Four? I don't know if he is after you or just trying to destroy me and my accomplishments. Either way puts you in danger. So, just as a precaution, I burned the papers. The less he knows about you, the better." He looked longingly at the front door and added quietly. "For both of you."

I was quiet for a moment, remembering my escape attempt. "What exactly does the salt do? When you try to cross it, that is."

In the slits of moonlight that fell across his face, I saw a deep frown nestle upon him. "I'm afraid you'll find out soon enough."

# Chapter Fifteen:

# Officially Insane

I would have sat there all night if I could. The quiet of the night, mixing with the comforting smells of the kitchen and the knowledgeable company I shared it with. I hadn't noticed my eyelids drooping until Saxe prodded me. My eyes flew open, and I jumped clean into the air.

"About time for me to retire. I suggest you do the same," Saxe said, smiling up at me.

I floated down and nodded, rubbing sleep from my eyes.

As I watched him climb the stairs, I noticed a weariness that hadn't been there when Lyla and I first met him. Every step was loaded with exhaustion. Each stair gave him fits. His shoulders drooped, and his face sagged from stress and fatigue. I wondered hazily if we were the cause of that. Being cooped up with us for a month couldn't be easy.

I climbed into bed and just threw a sheet over me. I was out before my head hit the pillow.

. . .

I was vaguely aware of Lyla and Saxe standing in the doorway. I wanted to stay comfortably cool and naive under my sheet. They were talking about something, but I didn't care. I heard Lyla take two giant steps forward before launching herself at me. She sailed through the air and landed on top of me. My eyes flew open. I groaned on impact and rolled over. She laughed and shook my shoulders. "Get up!" she said.

I heard Saxe chuckle from the door.

"Was this your idea?" I asked, pulling a sheet up to cover my face.

"No, Lyla's. But I have to admit, I got just as much enjoyment out of it as she did."

I groaned. I wished my eyes would adjust to the bright sunlight streaming through the window so I could glare at both of them. Lyla still sat on top of me when I peeked out from under the sheets. She looked at me expectantly.

"What?" I said before pushing her off of me. I sat up and looked at them. They smiled back at me. "Really, what?" Did I have something on me? I ran my fingers through my hair, it stood up at odd angles, but that was nothing new. I brushed off my face but found nothing.

Lyla giggled. "We've got a surprise for you."

She waddled back over me and pulled me up and out of bed. Then I saw her clothes. She wore a pretty lace dress with ruffles near the bottom and her hair had a ribbon in the back. She looked beautiful, but I knew something was up. She never dressed up just for the fun of it.

She let go of my hand and ran in front of me. She threw her hands wide and said, "Ta-da!"

I couldn't help but marvel at the transformation. When I went to bed last night, the kitchen looked the same as it always did. The cabinets were made of intricate branches, the island was smooth stone, the flowers added splashes of color.

Now, the kitchen was vibrant with color. Banners of flowers spelled my name. The island had an intricate tablecloth over it. Breakfast was strewn across it. And best of all, there wasn't a glass of orange juice in sight. Across the room, there was a sizable floating mirror that I had definitely never seen before.

"Thank you so much, but what's the occasion?"

"Well, over the years, we've celebrated a few of my birthdays with flowers or a stolen cupcake. But we've never celebrated one of yours. I know, I know, you don't know the exact date. But why not do it today? You've been through so much recently, so we thought we'd lighten the mood a little."

I blinked back tears. "Thank you, both of you."

Lyla ran forward and wrapped me in a hug. Saxe stood nearby, but I reached out an arm. "Come on, old man," As we embraced, a thought bounced around in my head, *I think I'm going to enjoy the next few days.* I chuckled. *I had to be insane to believe that.*

"Go change, then we'll eat."

"I can eat in these the same way I could in anything else."

"Just trust me."

I walked into our room and, like magic, there were clothes on my bed. The sheets were made up, and the pillow was fluffed. I slipped on the dress pants and the suspenders. There was a comb there too. I didn't want to, but for Lyla, I tamed the beast. I walked out from behind the door with a grimace. Lyla clapped. "You look great," she said, eyeing my hair.

"Before you sit down, we want to give you our gifts."

"Gifts?" Were plural gifts part of a typical birthday? Had I been doing Lyla's wrong all these years?

Lyla handed me a package. "Just be gentle with it," she said as I tore off the twine around it. I carefully peeled back the brown paper. Inside the box was a homemade cake. My name was spelled out in all capital letters with birthday and happy in fancy lettering above it and below it. Berries adorned the sides, and candied flowers added to the color scheme.

"Thank you," I said, putting it gently back on the table.

Unlike Lyla, Saxe didn't hand me a box or an envelope. He took us over to the mirror system. "This is going to sound strange, but smile at the mirror."

"Okay? Just smile?"

"Yes, and hold it, please."

Lyla stood to my right, and Saxe was to my left. Our smiling and unmoving reflections stared back at us. Saxe smiled absent-mindedly. He stared into the mirror for a long second, then closed his eyes. "Paper," he said, extending his hand. I looked around, but Lyla had already handed him some.

I watched as he transformed the blank square into a

colorful and a very familiar shape. The paper floated there as

he moved his fingers in complicated patterns around it. Pieces

of things around the room began flying around. Petals of

flowers came forward to give color to the picture. A bit of

cake icing, a scrap of Lyla's lace, a strand of my hair.

Everything hit the paper at once. Once finished, he smiled

and brushed off the excess. When he handed it back to me, it

was a picture of us. There we were, all standing in a line,

smiling. "Thank you," I said in awe.

"Now, how about some food?"

We ate and chatted, but I couldn't help but stare at

the picture we had just taken. It had captured us perfectly.

Lyla was slightly in front of me, but she had shifted to look at

me at the last second. She was smiling fondly up at me. I had

my hand protectively on her shoulder. Saxe stood beside me,

a slight smile on his face. Behind us, the kitchen was

displayed in all its glory. I saw the love in Saxe's eyes as he gazed at me through the paper. I slipped it into my pocket with a smile.

I could taste the time they had poured into the meal. The love flowing between us was tangible and genuine. I knew just how much I was needed and loved among the people in my company. I felt guilty thinking about how much I had wanted to escape this morning.

I could see the excitement in Lyla's face when we sliced her cake. The vanilla icing and sprinkled icing sugar added to the overall goodness.

They may have been celebrating me, but the day was for all of us.

We played games I'd never heard of, Saxe performed a few magic tricks for us. But my favorite part of the day was when we just chatted. We talked, not necessarily about heavy subjects or the days looming ahead of us, like old friends. I have never had an adult treat me with respect and understand my problems. Anyone I've ever talked to for longer than two minutes was either trying to convert me or arrest me.

"Then, Cole swooped down with the ham under his shirt. He grabbed a mop and put it on his head, and draped a few tablecloths around him. When the police ran past, they thought he was a pregnant woman!" Lyla said, finishing her story with a laugh.

We all shared her laugh. Saxe had tears squeezing out of the corners of his eyes. "Ugliest woman they'd ever seen!" I joked.

He shook his head and wiped the tear away with his forefinger. "It's just nice to have this old house echo with laughter for a change."

Lyla smiled at him. I started to smile at him, but I couldn't get around an image that had just popped into my mind. Lyla kept talking with him while my mind explored the idea further.

Saxe had been alone since he left home all those years ago. Nothing to give him hope for a better future. New visions warning of a coming danger, the threat of an invasion hanging over his head.

All alone, day after day, night after night, with no one to talk with when he woke in a cold sweat. No one to theorize with after seeing the Four.

Then, like the dawn breaking after a winter night, he receives a new vision. A boy and a girl in need. Finally, he'll have company. He'll have someone to help bear his burdens. I could always see the love in his eyes, but I had never understood why it was there. We saved him from years of loneliness. River Haven wasn't empty anymore, the spare room was full, the kitchen smelled of home. The yard was filled with trampled grass from our games.

As much as I loved Lyla, there was a level of love and gratitude I would never understand sitting next to me. I could witness it radiating from every inch of Saxe's body.

I smiled at him and joined them in conversation again. I had never felt more at ease or more comfortable with him. The ties of familial love had finally bound us together.

# Chapter Sixteen:

## Morning of Madness

I woke that dreaded morning still in a state of denial. The past month had been incredible. We ate together for every meal. We had gone to bed every night only after watching the stars fade into existence. Last night we opened the front window to watch the rain that fell in steady torrents.

Why did the air this morning seem laced with poison? Tension was high, and nerves were on edge. I swung my legs over the bed. Once my feet hit the floor, I remembered why today felt so malicious. Tonight, the blood moon would rise in the sky and drag us into a battle for our lives.

I took the salt jar out from under my bed and checked the window. The line appeared intact, but I thickened it. A little more couldn't hurt. I stowed the salt and walked into the kitchen. As always, I emerged to find Lyla's smiling face. But today, it looked pained. Saxe ordinarily would be standing over the stove keeping breakfast warm. Today he was in the chair beside her. He looked as if he hadn't slept in a week. His shoulders drooped, and his breathing labored. Today I saw just how hollow his cheeks were. His chestnut beard had thinned and grayed. Once, it was neatly trimmed and close cut, but now it was thinning and uneven. I must have chosen to ignore the obvious signs of wear over the past weeks. Today the sight hit me with fresh pain.

I sighed. "Today's the day," I said. I knelt in front of him and put a hand on his knee. "After tonight, this will all be over. One way or another." Lyla searched my eyes for comfort and answers I didn't have.

"Anything new?" he asked quietly.

I shook my head. Nothing had changed in my dreams, not even a single detail.

I patted his hand, trying to comfort him. "You might have a better vantage point from your study. Can I help you up there?"

He nodded. He put a hand on my shoulder as he pushed himself up. Lyla smiled gently up at him as she took his other arm. We ascended the stairs carefully and as evenly as we could. I caught a glimpse of his bedroom as we passed. The door was only open a crack, but I saw that it was unusually messy. Books and pages lay everywhere. The sheets and pillows were thrown across the bed in tangles. I tore my eyes away from the disheveled bedroom as we entered the Library. We lowered Saxe into the chair by the window.

"I'll go make some tea," Lyla offered.

I leaned on the windowsill and stared out the glass for a moment before swinging it wide. "You might need a breeze," I explained without looking at him. "And it will look more natural. Gives us the element of surprise." I chuckled halfheartedly.

I looked back at him, expecting a smile of recognition. He was smiling, but tears brimmed in his eyes.

"Don't go all sentimental on me," I said with a smile. "You can do that afterward." I put my hands on my hips and deepened my voice. "Cole, you've done such an excellent job. Those vigils didn't stand a chance against us!" I smiled, but he only shook his head sadly.

"I couldn't have asked for a better person to be my heir." He said quietly. "Cole, no matter what happens today, I want you to know that I am proud of you. I'm proud of the man you are becoming and of the young woman you've raised." He took a shuttering breath and blinked hard. "You make flaws look seamless. Your magic is increasing daily, and your capacity for learning and understanding has never been larger. Keep studying. Someday, you will go far. Years from now, you are going to make a huge difference in this shattered world of ours."

I smiled sadly and shook my head. "Thanks, old man, but keep your life-altering speech for afterward. Then we will have the rest of our lives to talk."

He smiled at me, but his eyes yielded a sadness I could never take away from him. Lyla came in with a steaming cup of tea. She handed it to him, guiding it with a gentle hand. After only a few sips, life seemed to seep back into him.

"Why don't you both go check the salt and make sure we haven't broken it anywhere? Don't worry about tonight. We cannot deal with it right now. We will just fight that battle when it comes to us."

We rushed out to do as we were told.

My curiosity got the better of me. As Lyla descended the stairs, I slipped into Saxe's bedroom. I stepped over his traveling cloak and around papers strewn in every direction. Books lay in various positions. His notebook lay on the bed, deflated and lifeless. I knew the ripped pieces everywhere must be the missing pages. Why had he tossed them out? Why were some words scribbled out while others weren't? If he was so ready to destroy the notebook, why didn't he just burn it?

I checked the salt line by the window and found it intact. I exited the room as quietly as I had entered.

I met Lyla at the base of the stairs. I saw the questions and the speculations forming in her eyes, but I ignored them. "Have you looked at all the windows?"

"Yes, and the front door." A moment of silence yawned between us. "Cole, when you said 'one way or another,' what exactly did you mean?" She didn't meet my eyes. This had been eating at her all morning. She feared the worst, and I didn't have the heart to lie again.

I sat down on the bottom step and sighed. "I don't know enough about magic to be certain, but why would his condition get any better if we ward off this army? What's stopping his brother from hitting River Haven again and again and again?" I didn't have to say that Saxe had a plan he wasn't telling us. I could see it in her eyes, she was just as worried as I was. I wasn't sure what he knew, but he refused to tell us.

Lyla blinked hard. "So, you're saying tonight is the first of many?"

I nodded. "And it's going to be a long night."

She turned the corner to the sunroom, trying to hide her grim expression. I silently ascended the stairs. When I peeked in, Saxe was staring out the window and at the mountains beyond.

The last few days, he had primarily drawn to himself. Yesterday I had ascended the stairs with a question. I paused in the doorway, my hand hovering in front of the wood grain. I could hear a faint whimpering behind the door. When I peeked inside, his back was to me. His hands were on his head, and his fingers were knotted in his hair. His eyes were squeezed shut in concentration. I was terrified he would hear me and turn around as I hurried back down the stairs. I waited in the kitchen, unsure of what to do. I counted to ten before tromping up the stairs more loudly. When I knocked on the door, he opened it with a smile.

He kept himself together so well. Only when he thought he was alone did he let any emotion show. When he was quiet in his bedroom at night, I knew he was falling apart. I desperately wanted to help him, but I couldn't find the right words to say or the spell to use. Even so, I could still see a glimmer of hope in his eyes when I entered a room unexpectedly. He watched us with pride. His voice thickened with emotion more frequently than it used to.

I knocked softly. "Sir?"

"They will be coming from there." He said, gesturing towards the mountains.

"How can you tell?"

"There's smoke coming from just beyond them. I expect the army will be visible within the next hour."

"When will they get here?" Lyla asked, trying to hide the tremor in her voice.

"Just before sundown."

"In all the visions I've had, the moon has been full and already in the sky."

"Like I said, time is a strange variable in these things."

I steeled myself for the worst and finally asked, "What's our plan?"

"Hide, outlast their patience."

"Where? This is a small cottage, and I don't want to hide somewhere without both of you."

"Up here," he reached out and pulled an invisible rope. A square of the ceiling transformed into steep stairs.

"Woah," I breathed.

"I'll take my time getting up there. You two should go downstairs and make the bedroom look like no one was ever there."

He rose shakily and walked towards the stairwell. I stepped forward to help, but he waved me away.

I walked tentatively back towards the door, keeping an eye on him. He inched his way up the ladder-like stairs. I followed Lyla downstairs and towards our room, lending my ear to the ceiling. Hoping against hope I wouldn't hear a terrible thud. With my mind still on the unknown attic above me, I continued down the stairs.

I turned the corner to find a shadowy figure standing in the middle of the kitchen. Lyla continued walking into our room, oblivious or blind to the visitor. I watched him poke around. He inspected the salt and the sturdiness of our windows and doors. While he looked around the sunroom, he stiffened as if sensing my gaze. He turned around and looked me dead in the eye. I couldn't make out most of his features, but I saw his fists clench. I balled my own, expecting him to charge.

He swooped his arm dramatically and touched the floor. As he brought it up again, every part of his body disintegrated into dust. With a single swish, he was gone. This had felt different from every other vision I had seen. I had still been able to see Lyla during the episode. In my previous visions, I wasn't. Was this a sign that I was improving? Or was this encounter unique in another way?

I rolled the image of the boy dissolving into a puff of smoke around in my head. I joined Lyla. She was folding clothes and creating stacks on the bed. I grabbed the picture Saxe had given me and tucked it into my pocket. I put the book on my bed and began piling the clothes on top of it. Lyla's clothes were all neatly folded and evenly aligned. Mine mismatched and stuck out at odd angles. I made up the bed and fluffed the pillow to get out the head-shaped indentation.

I dug around under my bed to find the shoes I had kicked under. I hadn't ever worn them, but it was the thought that counts.

"Cole?" said a quiet voice from behind me. I turned to see Lyla staring intently at me. I froze. "What's our next step from here?"

"We will stay in the attic for a while," I answered matter of factly.

"What if they find us?"

"I don't think they will, the rope is invisible, and I'll put some counter spells in place. I'm sure Saxe has a hundred running today. That's why he's so tired."

"If worse comes to worst, and we have to fight hand to hand, could you ever forgive me for joining?"

"Have you ever used a weapon before?"

"Yes, but that's not what I'm asking. I know you

well enough; you'll try to lock me up in the attic to watch as you become a martyr. Would you forgive me for disobeying and fighting by your side anyway?"

I swallowed hard. I could afford damage to this house and even myself. If that man laid so much as a finger on Lyla, he had another thing coming. My whole world would collapse if anything happened to her. "Yes," I answered finally.

She smiled faintly. "Good, because I would have done it even if you said no."

# Chapter Seventeen:

# Arrival

After carrying up our own things, we brought up several things Saxe had asked for. Food, some medical supplies, and a few blankets. I pulled myself up through the tiny door for the last time and swung my legs up into the attic. Saxe closed up the trapdoor, and we waited. I laid on my back and watched the circle-shaped window cast odd reflections onto the ceiling. Saxe sank into a silence during which he only stared at the mountainside. Lyla fiddled with the hem of her pants before reading the book of spells, incantations, and potions. I could see the concern creeping into her eyes. I handed her the worn book on poetry. A brief smile crossed her face as she flipped through the familiar pages.

I saw her take a nub of a pencil from behind her ear

and scribble in the margins. Somehow, this is what snapped Saxe out of his daze. He pulled a paper from one of his various pockets. She smiled and was again submerged into her world of words and rhymes. I watched her plot out rhyme schemes and multiple rhythms. A reminder for iambic pentameter was scribbled on the left corner.

Saxe and I watched her with a smile as she turned mud into moonlight and fate into a game. He turned from her and back towards the window. The smile melted from his face. I got up to look at the army's progression. They were at the base of the mountain now. The only thing between us now was rolling hills.

"You have a plan?" I asked.

"Obviously," he joked.

"Want to share it?"

The glint in his eyes had returned. "Let our defenses

do what they do best. When they are finally inside, remain silent until further action is required."

"Rather vague, don't you think?"

"All of the best plans are."

I rolled my eyes. "You've finally gone crazy, old man."

He smiled and let his gaze finally drift back over to the window. I glanced out the window with him. The grass under the apple tree began to writhe and move. "What the-" I started as we both leaned forward. A huge hole opened up, and a boy leapt out. "Holy-Did you see that?"

"My eyes *do* work."

"I need to learn that one."

"However cool it may look, it puts us in jeopardy."

"Maybe he was just sent to scope it out."

"That's my point. What's stopping that boy from

leaving that open and letting every soldier through right now?"

I felt a surge of fear. "How much time do we have?"

"An hour tops."

"Is now a bad time to mention I saw a shadow in our kitchen earlier?"

"Really there or a vision?"

"I think it was foretelling this. He just looked around this cottage."

"I don't think it could be right now."

"Why not?"

"He's leaving."

I moved to see him more clearly. He was walking back towards the hole. He swept the grounds with one final gaze before dropping back into the depths from which he came.

"Oh. Well then. That muddies up the 'when' question, doesn't it?" I said. I felt the vast expanse of waiting left for me. I sat down on the edge of his rocking chair and kept my eyes glued to the window.

"How's the vision game coming? I've heard you two laughing late in the night."

Lyla shut her book. "It's incredible, Mr. Saxe. He's terrific."

I sighed as Saxe raised his eyebrows at me. "Is that so? Will you demonstrate for us?"

I close my eyes with a smile. I squeezed my eyes shut and emptied my mind. I held up a hand with three fingers. I counted down and pointed at the window with a dramatic flair. A leaf fell in front of the window.

Lyla playfully hit my arm. "You can do better than that!"

"Give me a break! Nothing exciting is happening in the next few seconds. And it takes me a minute to clear my mind."

"Why don't you guess what word I'll say?"

Saxe smiled encouragingly. I closed my eyes and saw Lyla's lips forming a word.

"Acorn!" We shouted in unison.

"Church."

"Bath."

I turned to face Saxe when I foresaw his comment coming. "I'll stop you right here. I smell fine, thank you!"

# Chapter Eighteen:

## Non-Negotiable

Half an hour later, the mystery boy reappeared. He jumped from a hole in the middle of the yard, in full view of our window. After a quick look around, he beckoned an army out of the darkness. The sun was at its peak, only moments away from beginning its fall back towards earth.

Every soldier lined up in front of River Haven. "What are they doing?" I whispered. "They aren't even trying to hide their numbers." I paused, considering their battle plans. "They aren't surrounding us or attacking us." I got up and moved closer to the window. "Are they just going to stand there?"

"Mark Saxe," a voice echoed from everywhere. I could barely make out the lips of the front thug moving. The shadowy boy had his hand on the thug's shoulder. "Surrender yourself and everything in your possession. Come peacefully, and no harm will come to you." Lyla and I looked at him, unsure of how he could respond.

He closed his eyes and stood up.

"You're not going to do it, are you? You know they have to be lying!"

He ignored me and began muttering. His hands move symmetrically around as he casts unseen protective barriers. I saw a faint blue hovering around the borders of the house.

"I am no fool, Cole," he said with a small smile. He sat back down and looked out the window.

"We'll give you a quarter of an hour to think it over and deliver yourself to us. If you haven't appeared by then, we will come in forcefully and remove you."

Saxe revealed a genuine smile. "I'd love to see them try."

I chuckled. A weight was lifted from my shoulders. If he could joke and poke fun, then he couldn't be that worried. Right?

Lyla grinned, "They'll never even get to the salt. They'll be too busy running in fear."

"We'll just sit pretty up here all day, while they break their backs trying to-Good gravy!" I jumped back. A face had appeared in the window. It was outlined by the setting sun, so I couldn't make out any of its features. But it was there as plain as day. I clamped a hand over Lyla's mouth to stop a scream that never came.

He peered inside but didn't seem to see us. He turned and was gone. Lyla peeled my hand off of her face with a glare.

"He-he didn't see us," I said, dumbfounded.

"Did you really think I would not protect my windows?"

"It slipped my mind," I muttered. Another thought popped into my head. "If this is your brother's doing, where is he?"

He gave a weak smile. "He's too paranoid to show himself before the actual battle has begun."

"Then who's the boy wizard?"

"Could be an apprentice or a son."

"Son?" Lyla asked, getting up to look for herself.

"My brother always seemed to appeal to women. Perhaps he finally got married."

I shuddered. "Who would want to marry a murderous creep?"

"Who wouldn't?" Lyla quipped. She sat back down

and continued flipping through her book again.

Saxe and I looked at one another before turning our attention back to the window. "How long do you think they'll wait before attacking?"

"A quarter of an hour."

"You think they'll stay true to their word?"

"Why wouldn't they?"

"Why *would* they?"

As we watched, a group of thugs came together to plan a coordinated attack. After a moment of discussion, they broke away from the group and walked to opposite sides of the houses.

"They're surrounding us," I breathed.

"They are looking for an unguarded way in."

They formed a loose line all the way around the cottage. One man picked up a handful of dirt and threw it at the wall. It blew towards the house and hit the stone wall harmlessly. I saw the man gesturing to his small experiment and speaking with the boy. The dark boy only shook his head and began moving his hands in rough circular motions. Dirt hovered in front of him in a crude ball. With a violent heave, he sent it barreling towards the cottage. It bounced off an invisible force field and buried the man beside the boy. The boy turned away from the struggling man and walked back to the apple tree.

"They don't look very unified."

"They'll charge as one, attack from all sides."

"What if they get inside?"

He was silent.

"Saxe, what's the plan if they get inside?"

A deafening roar exploded outside as our allotted time ticked to a close. The battle had begun.

They pounded against the cottage, but each punch, arrow, or sword, bounced off harmlessly. Even the Pixie returned to serve its vengeance. It caused mayhem and chaos through their ranks. The Pixie became brave enough to challenge the boy himself. The boy seemed to be the head of the army, despite his age. He stood silently at the base of the tree, watching his army fail utterly. He didn't flinch as the bright streak of light came at him, instead he crushed the Pixie without a second thought.

He continued to watch from a distance as his men were slaughtered by their own swords bouncing back into them. One man fired arrow after arrow at the windows, but they bounced harmlessly off. One arrow seemed to penetrate the surface of the force field for an instant before falling to the ground. Saxe grimaced and groaned with every strike.

"Stop," I muttered under my breath.

When the boy finally raised his hand over his head for the onslaught to cease, he sucked in a relieved breath. He brought his hand down, and a clap of thunder broke through the valley. Rocks flew through the air and collided with the barrier. Saxe cried out in pain.

"Stop. Stop it!" I told no one in particular. "Just let the barriers fall. We can take the handful of them left."

He shook his head. "Not yet."

Lyla closed her eyes against the sight of him writhing in pain. Blow after blow hit until they began to rattle the windows. With a final gasp, the barrier fell. A rock sailed through a window in the sunroom. I saw pleasure change the boy's posture.

Saxe was beginning to steady his breathing when a figure stepped out from behind the apple tree. The man looked just like Saxe. Except for his thinning dark hair shining in the fading light. His robes were moth-eaten and dusty. The man spoke only to the boy. The boy's posture was stiff and rigid as the evil Saxe look alike gave him orders.

He looked up at the window where we cowered. His eyes met mine and a cruel smile spread across his face. The man stepped behind the tree and disappeared again. Saxe and I took a collective breath of relief.

"Why don't you recover your strength and hit them from a distance?" I suggested, worrying for his life on the battlefield. "I'll go down and distract them, maybe you can both escape, and I'll join you later."

I got up, ignoring Saxe's quiet pleas for me to stay. I paused at the trapdoor. I heard a yell from downstairs as the first thug discovered why salt was a formidable weapon. I jumped down the trapdoor and into Saxe's office.

# Chapter Nineteen:

# Trapped

I turned to close the trapdoor just as Lyla jumped after me. She landed on top of me with a heavy thud. We hit the floor hard and tangled into odd positions. She tried to get up off of me. "Sorry, sorry, I thought you saw me."

I got up and stretched my aching back. "I thought you were going to stay and help Saxe."

She twirled her staff, ready for action. "Did you forget already? I'm coming with you."

"No, I need you to stay up there."

"You *want* me up there. You *need* me to guard your back."

I wanted to argue, but the ensuing crash from downstairs cut me off.

"Fine, follow me." We began making our way out of the study as the trap door closed itself behind us. She clutched her staff and stayed right on my tail. We snuck down the stairs and peeked around the corner. A rock the size of my head had crashed through the kitchen window. Salt scattered everywhere, and our barrier was broken. Two thugs were struggling through the wreckage. My eyes widened as I witnessed the house defend itself. The branches that held the glass in place began to writhe and form a window without glass. The men jumped back, alarmed.

I waved Lyla on, we bunkered in the sunroom and waited for the inevitable. Another rock crashed through the window. The thugs struggled through the opening before the vines and branches had a chance to reform. I turned to look at her. Her eyes looked terrified, but she held her staff at the ready. "When they turn the corner, we attack. Okay?" I

whispered.

"Why don't we wait until there are more? We can hit more at the same time?" she mouthed.

"What if we get overwhelmed?" I whispered back, trying to keep an eye on the front door.

"Good point."

We waited for the thugs to walk towards the stairs. When their backs were turned, we hit them simultaneously. I thrust them back towards the door while Lyla blinded them with a rainstorm. I beckoned the front door to open, and they stumbled through. The salt was undisturbed, so I closed the door again and silently celebrated our small victory.

To the men outside, the attacks were strange and unavoidable magic. They kept coming in pairs. Some swung wildly with their swords. Others battled at the air, as if that would help. Lyla gave me a grin every time we sent them running out the front door. We stayed hidden in the sunroom, but the thug's heavy boots were easy enough to hear coming.

We waited for our new pair of victims to come around the corner. I kept my hands balled into fists. Lyla's knuckles were white from gripping the staff. There was a long silence. They either stopped sending soldiers in, or the boy was reevaluating their entry plan. I looked around the corner, and my breath caught. The silhouette of the boy now stood in the doorway. He was obviously trained in magical arts. I was full of nervous energy. I clenched my fists and waited for him to round the corner. He sauntered steadily forward, taking in every inch of the cottage.

Perhaps if I had waited for just a second longer, things would have been different. Maybe if I hadn't shifted my feet or taken a steadying breath, he would have remained oblivious. I acted on impulse, just as I had with the thugs. I sent a gust of wind to push him down.

This time, he didn't move. A laugh echoed from an unseen voice. The boy's form in the kitchen flickered like a dying candle and vanished. He reappeared in the doorway and beckoned the other thugs in. He turned to look at us one last time before disappearing. He didn't reappear in the yard. He was gone.

We had given ourselves away. *I* had given us away. I pushed Lyla further into the room. "We need to get out of here!" I hissed, keeping my eye on the kitchen.

"I don't want to leave Mr. Saxe!"

"Then we'll go out these windows and go around!"

"We can't just lead them to Mr. Saxe!"

"Then we need a better plan," I hissed, peeking around the corner. A thug saw me and came running into the sunroom. He swung his knife, but I ducked. He hit the doorframe, and the blade stuck.

"Run!" I shouted. He struggled to pry the dagger back out of the wood. He left a large notch in Saxe's beautifully carved doorway.

We turned and ran for the nearest window. I sent a shock of air and busted the glass. While clamoring out the window, I scattered as much of the salt as I could because I didn't want to be trapped outside. We kept running for tree cover. I turned to see the thugs rearranging themselves and a moment later, two archers appeared. I grabbed Lyla's hand and took off into the air.

Arrows now protruded from the ground where we had just stood. We floated onto the roof and heaved a sigh of relief.

She hugged me and began to stand up when another arrow came sailing overhead. I jerked her back down and sent a gust of wind to knock it aside.

These were trained archers. I couldn't avoid them for long. We slid along the shingles that tore and grabbed at our clothes and exposed fingers, down along the slanted part of the roof until we reached a tower that contained Saxe's bedroom, study, and the secret attic. I heard an arrow whispering towards us. I closed my eyes and stuck out a hand. I braced for impact, but nothing came. I opened my eyes and found that the wind had acted as an extension of my hand. I made the motion of throwing the arrow, and the wind copied me. "Thanks," I said as I floated down to the window. I shielded my eyes, trying to see inside. I couldn't catch sight of Saxe, but maybe he replaced the enchantments after all.

I banged on the window, but the moment I touched the glass pane a green fire erupted from the window. I jerked back, but it lept towards me. I was engulfed in seconds. The smoke filled my mouth and eyes. I thrashed and swatted at them, but they refused to be doused. I couldn't focus on hovering, and I began to fall from the air. I grabbed onto the window sill with one hand. I dangled dangerously above a team of thugs, ready to catch me and promptly stab me if I fell. An arrow pierced my dangling arm, blood instantly trickled down to my fingers. Lyla reached out to help me.

"Get back!" I yelled, trying to pat myself off with my unoccupied hand. I didn't want her to burn as well. I also didn't want her to witness my death. She jerked backward, and I lost sight of her.

I tried, for her sake, to keep quiet. Every inch of me was being bitten by the fangs of the fire. It never seemed to burn away my clothes or skin, but it felt like they had reached the bone.

A hand touched the window, and the burning

stopped. I might have fallen back to the ground if Saxe hadn't caught me. I coughed and spluttered.

"Where's Lyla?" He asked.

I pointed with my bloodied arm. Saxe grabbed my other hand and hauled me to sit on the window sill. I put a hand to where the arrow stuck out of my arm and yanked. I bit my bottom lip and pressed my hand to the wound to stem the bleeding.

"Both of you, get in here now. I have a plan."

"Oh, now you do?" I said between clenched teeth

He smiled apologetically.

I nodded, and he let go. I swooped up over the roof to celebrate, but the sight of Lyla caught in my throat. She was doubled over an arrow, tears trickling down her face.

"I-I'm sorry," she choked. I dropped down beside her, afraid to move. "I didn't see it coming."

I inched closer to get a better look. She had her fingers against the place of impact, trying to keep pressure on it. Blood oozed out from between her fingers and stained her shirt. I put my hand on it as well. She grimaced. I eased her onto my lap so I could cradle her like I always had when she was younger.

She pulled it out with a cry of pain. Her precious blood was everywhere. I lifted her shirt a few inches. It was deep. Too deep to mean anything good. I pressed my hand to her abdomen, and she grimaced. A raven flew overhead and took an arrow that may have hit one of us. Every spell I'd ever practiced or even read about flitted through my mind. "You're going to be okay," I promised, choking back tears. I closed my eyes and began mumbling. She slid her hand out from under mine and placed it tenderly on my face. I opened my eyes to look at her. She shook her head sadly. I grabbed her hand and squeezed it. "You will be," she promised, wincing as she spoke.

"*We* will be. Won't we?" I clutched her as her life slipped between my fingers. She gasped in pain as more arrows rained down on us. "Stop," I muttered, my eyes fixed on her. More arrows came, missing us by inches. "Stop it!" I screamed down at them.

"You're going to be okay," I promised again. The lie seemed to cut me even as I said it.

"Keep talking, Cole." She squeezed her eyes shut. "Please."

I nodded and racked my brain. "After this, we're going to Rolling Acres. The only thing in the country is the mountains. Right now, I bet those peaks are just dripping in color. There will be valleys full of nothing but wildflowers. You could roam for miles and not find another person. We'll make ourselves a little house and plant some food. Then, when the winter comes, we'll sit out on our back porch and watch the snow fall slowly from Silver Point. There won't be anyone to chase us, or hunt us down." She smiled faintly as she smoothed a wrinkle in my shirt. The expression froze on her face as her gaze grew distant. "We'll be free."

My heart seemed to stop beating. "Lyla?" I said, shaking her shoulders. "Lyla!" I huddled over her, trying to keep her warmth from fleeing.

I threw the arrow away as if that could make a difference. I cradled her close, trying to shield her from the raining arrows. An arrow bit into my leg as I dodged one aimed for my shoulder. It took every ounce of strength I had to stand up and leave her there. I knew the archers would find a way onto the roof and keep firing until they did. I could hear her voice as if she were standing next to me.

*Go,* she would whisper. *There's nothing you can do for me now.*

I turned and flew for the window. I tumbled over the window sill and slammed it shut. Arrows shattered the pane behind me.

"Where's Lyla?" Saxe asked as he helped me up.

I hung my head. "We'll meet her later." Saxe turned his head. "I'm so sorry, Cole. I wish it didn't have to happen like this."

"Yeah," I muttered. "I'm sure we both do." I sat in the corner as Saxe began pacing. I pulled my knees up and rested my forehead in them.

If Lyla were here, she'd be right next to me, comforting me. She'd tell me that it was all going to work out or that things look darkest just before the light.

But it was silent as the grave. No one said what

needed to be spoken. Not even Saxe could find the words to say. He wept silently in the corner, hands covering his face. I stored up all the unspoken words in my heart, wishing in vain for Lyla's quiet voice.

I closed my eyes and tried not to think. I was flooded with images of her thin frame, almost nine years old, grinning from ear to ear. For weeks, I had stolen bits of fabric to sew together a doll for her. I smiled, thinking of how her eyes had brightened when I revealed it to her.

The following year I snuck into a cart that we had found on the side of the road. I had stolen a picture book and a book of poems. Those lines and rhymes had shaped and molded her mind into a bit of a poet herself. After years of pointing out street signs and shop names, she'd learned how to read. I gave her every scrap of information I could wring from my mind. Using newspapers to trace and practice, she had taught herself to write in small, simple sentences.

I would wake to see her staring into a barren orchard or up into the clear sky most misty mornings. I saw trees and sky, but she saw the promise of a world that could be. She saw the world through a lens that was all her own. From rays of sunlight and dots of color on the side of the road, she would craft something incredible. Her rhythm and symbolism were her way of grasping reality. Her rhyme schemes were her road maps to who she wanted to become. She could write mud into a masterpiece.

Reality slammed into me like a runaway train. Lyla would never watch the sunrise with teary eyes. I would never feel her hand in mine. The absence of her warmth beside me was a hollow reminder of the distance between us now.

Saxe cleared his throat, and I finally looked up. "Ready?" His voice trembled along with his hands.

I took one last long look at the empty place next to me before standing. I wiped my face and nodded.

# Chapter Twenty:

## Final Resting Places

Thugs began beating on the door downstairs. He bent down and locked the trapdoor. "That hasn't been locked this whole time?" I asked.

"I was preoccupied."

"With what?"

"Never-you-mind. I have one last spell that might get rid of them. I need you to fly outside and distract them. But try to trap as many inside as you can."

"What spell will you be doing?"

"A complicated one. Now, let me concentrate." He closed his eyes. I started for the window.

"No!" he called suddenly. He looked at me in fear. "They've set the house on fire."

"How can you tell?

"*I* am the one who keeps this house up. The tree that forms the kitchen cabinets, walls, and the floor we kneel on would have died long ago if not for me."

"Then we need to move faster."

He nodded.

I leaped back out the window and tried to push the grief away for a moment. I called out and looked around for the boy, but he was still nowhere to be found. I shot to kill and succeeded several times. I corralled them inside the kitchen and put up a barrier of air. I went back to the window and called for the wizard. I stepped inside to find him murmuring a spell. "Sir, please, we have to move!"

He didn't hear me. He opened his hands and let them fall to his side with one final whisper. He turned slowly, as if taking one last look at everything, but then he saw me.

"Cole? You shouldn't be here! I just-" the cottage lurched, stopping him short.

I grabbed his shoulder as we stumbled. "What was that? Did you do that?"

We stood up straighter and tried to keep our balance. "I've pulled my magic from the house. It will fall on the thug's heads within a matter of minutes." He paused and fixed his gaze on me. "It's going to collapse!" he repeated.

"But *we're* in the house!" I cried as we tumbled to a wall. Another load-bearing wall had fallen in.

"You weren't supposed to come back for me!" he cried.

I saw the pain in his eyes. Hurt that he had battled for years. Fear and uncertainty aside, this was the one thing he saw coming. "You said you have the gift of prophecy," I shouted over the clamor of voices and shouts of alarm rising from downstairs. "What about now makes you so scared? What did you see?"

His silence answered me.

"You think you die today?" I got in front of him, forcing him to look me in the eye. I saw every moment we'd shared flash through my mind. He showed the quiet love in so many forms.  From rescuing us in the alley to less flashy acts like making lunch, giving a comforting word, cooking and getting clothes, to just putting up with us in general, he had been the only father Lyla had never known.

I remembered laying awake all those nights, quaking in fear and losing sleep. Saxe had changed all that. He had taught me to laugh in the face of fear. He had pushed me to be a better brother, a better man, and a better magician.

"Don't let your fear control you!" I shouted with conviction. "Fight with everything you have!"

He had to fight. I knew that the instant I saw him lose hope, I would as well. Any hope of living past today had died on the roof only minutes ago. Any chance I had of surviving was left in him.

He took a deep breath, and his eyes shone with tears. "I will, Cole. But right now, you need to get out of this house." He pushed me towards the window.

I stumbled back, gripping his shirt. I knew my words were lost on deaf ears. His eyes showed me a world of pain and hopelessness, not only for himself but for me.

"I'm not leaving you behind!" I gasped as the voices escalated downstairs.

"Yes," he whispered as the last wall gave, "you are."

He pushed me backward with all the force he could muster. I knew the wind would catch me as I tumbled from the tower window, but I wanted it to take me back to him.

Instead, the wind listened to the last request of an old man. They kept me captive high enough to be safe from any arrows, but there weren't many men to fire them. When the cottage collapsed, it killed everything in it. I was trapped in reverent silence.

I roared in defiance. A power surge stronger then anything I'd ever felt swelled inside of me and melted the winds holding me back. I shot downward and hit the ground with a bone-shattering boom.

I gazed out across the rubble and barely stifled a sob. Nothing moved. The wind was still. Leaves were silent. The moon was high and drenched in blood. "Saxe!" I shouted. "Saxe! Lyla!" No one answered

I reached out my hand and closed my eyes, feeling for anything. "Bring me Lyla!" I begged. I heard something whoosh towards me. But it wasn't my baby sister's warm hand. My fingers closed around her staff. Everything in me wanted to break it in half and hurl it into the mountain, but something stopped me.

A little voice in the back of my mind whispered that this was all I had left of her.

I doubled my grip on it. "I promised," I muttered when I hit my knees. It was as though Lyla really was right next to me. Her walking stick had jumped to me, but even scarier was how right it felt in my hands. The bark didn't give me splinters or rub my hand. It wasn't too heavy or bottom-loaded.

It felt made for me.

I reared back to throw it across the valley. With it, I wanted to hurl the implications. Something stopped me. My chest tightened, and I dropped the staff to my side. I gripped it a little tighter and hit my knees.

"Saxe?" I called out in desperation. Something shifted in the rubble. My head snapped up. The last bit of hope I clung to was dashed when a book floated towards me. I slumped back again. What could a book do for my broken soul? When I picked it up, a piece of paper slipped out. It was written in Lyla's loopy, half-cursive handwriting.

It was a poem.

*If all of time is a book store*

*Don't you want to see inside?*

*You long to walk through the door,*

*With all its secrets and surprise.*

*But the Mender of books watches you.*

*He knows your deepest desires,*

*For He's read your book too,*

Only He knows what your story requires.

You can't see the end of your story

Because it's not your own.

To the Book Mender goes the glory,

For He wrote your tale alone.

Mending books is what He does best,

For you are His only love.

So when your sun is in the West,

He'll give you a little shove.

Since He's the author of your book,

Do not worry, and do not fret.

Give your life on second look,

*Because your Creator will never forget.*

*Judging a cover is wrong,*

*Remember who holds your pen.*

*It may not be very long*

*Before He writes The End.*

Notes about rewriting for iambic pentameter and more profound symbolism were scribbled on the sides. The words 'the end' were underlined. The rhyme scheme was scribed out to the side, and other possible rhyming words were listed. Every time the Book Mender was mentioned, either by name or by a pronoun, it was capitalized. I puzzled over this before flipping it over. It wasn't another poem but rather a short story. A letter that was never received.

*He may not have eyes deeper than amber or words*

more eloquent than a king. He doesn't have hands that work a mill or a hoe. He's all I've ever needed and all I've ever wanted. His chocolate hair and matching eyes couldn't hold a candle to the clearest of oceans, but his heart was mine. I've never felt safer than between his arms. Every breath he takes, and every beat of his heart is tuned to mine. He may only be my brother, but he has kept me alive for nearly thirteen years, and for that, I am eternally grateful.

Now it's my turn to give back. Cole, I love you. I love you beyond the reaches of time and past the stars. Happy Birthday.

I had to dry my eyes several times before I made it

through. I had failed her as a brother and a keeper of her well-being. I had broken the only promise I ever gave my mother. I couldn't keep her safe.

I had never been so alone. I had never hated loneliness as much as I did right now. All I wanted was the knowledgeable company of my sister and my guide. I wanted to speak with someone, anyone. I wanted to feel Lyla take my hand or Saxe ruffle my hair. What I wouldn't give to blink and do this day over again.

I opened my eyes to see a book in my lap. The same book I'd poured over only last night. The gift from Saxe. I flipped it open to the last page I'd read. The page just after 'The End'. Where last night there had only been a hundred blank pages, there were a hundred pages filled with new information. On the very first page, there was a handwritten note.

It read:

Cole,

If you're reading this, I'm dead. Don't feel sorry for me. I've seen this moment coming for many years. My only regret is that I couldn't prepare you for what's coming.

It's up to you to find the other three. Go four towns east, and wait until the next full moon. Find the place the four will gather and prepare for war.

Good luck to you, and remember to never lose hope,

MARK SAXE

The four? Was that what this was all about? I threw the book back into the rubble and stood up. My last remaining connection to this earth was gone. She'd helped me find my center. She had kept me bound to this life. Without her, I would have given up the day our parents left. Every time I

had gotten us kicked out of an orphanage, she had helped me

find a new one. Even the day I held her in the alleyway, she

had been the one tethering *me* to life. Without her, I would

have lost the light in my eyes well before now. Without her,

my life would have been over already.

I gritted my teeth and looked out over the rubble. I

couldn't leave her like this.

I couldn't find Saxe, but I found Lyla's body. It was

crumpled and cold. I chose a flat stone from the water's edge

where we had played in the river and I leaned it against the

oak tree. I began digging. I dug without an evident depth in

mind but stopped when I could barely jump out. It had been a

good, mind-numbing activity. One step at a time, just like

when we were young. One small thing leads to another. I

placed her in the bottom. I crossed her arms over her wound.

I closed her eyes and laid a flower in her hands, then sealed it with a kiss. I climbed out to say goodbye one last time.

I had been so prepared to die. So ready to walk hand in hand with her into whatever came next. I had never considered that it wouldn't be my body that died with Lyla but part of my spirit. A portion of me was buried with her, my hopes were locked in her unmoving heart. My hopes were lost in her unblinking eyes. My purpose dissipated with every clump of dirt I covered her with.

I sat at the base of the apple tree, not even caring to wipe the dirt from my hands. I leaned my head back onto the tree trunk. Maybe it was my imagination, but I thought I could hear something nearby. I could still smell smoke. Perhaps the boy was coming back to finish what he had started.

*Let him come,* I thought bitterly. I wouldn't even

raise a finger. I wouldn't protest. I wouldn't mumble a spell

or ask an element to come to my aid. I wanted to join them.

Let the boy made of smoke and lies come to do me a favor.

There was no way this was safe.

# Epilogue

No one came.

Hours passed.

Dawn came and went.

It took me a long time to gather the energy to move.

I poked through the rubble of the cottage. I found many of the men scattered among the wreckage, but I could find no sign of Saxe. It was as if he had never existed at all. I picked up the old book he had written for me and dusted off the leather-bound cover. I corrected the bent pages and smoothed the creases best I could.

He had spent his whole life preparing for the Four. His entire existence was meant to prepare a path for them, but he never got to see it come to fruition. How was I supposed to uphold that legacy?

I closed my eyes as I turned back to the apple tree.

Lyla's staff leaned against the stone I had buried her under. It felt wrong to take it, but I couldn't bear leaving it behind. Even with my eyes squeezed shut I could feel it sitting there, taunting me with it's magic. I could feel the tug in my gut. I opened my hand and it flew forward. I opened my eyes as it landed safely in my hand.

I took a running jump into the apple tree, staff clutched in one hand, book tucked under the other. I landed on the thinnest branch on the top of the boughs. I surveyed the land.

I could follow the sun in its decent West into the lands unknown and travel until my magic could take me no father. I could go north into Rolling Acres and wander Silver Point Mountain until my legs gave out. I could go South across the Calfkiller and follow Blue Spring Mountains into bandit territory. I glanced down at the corner of the paper sticking out from the book under my arm. Or, I could go East like the old man had wanted. I could risk my life for three total strangers and bring Saxe's prophecy into the light.

I blinked back tears as I watched the wind dance through the leaves around me. Lyla had been the only person I had loved and protected, but I had failed even that. The wind soared around me, ruffling my hair, and tousling my clothes. It pulled at the staff in my hand and swirled around my shoulders. It was as if Lyla were chastising me for thinking it.

A small smile tugged at my lips as the warm breeze brushed over me. I hadn't been able to protect Lyla, but this time I was a step ahead of my enemy. There was a chance the other three were still in the dark about the prophecy. I could protect them from this unknown threat. I may not have been able to keep Lyla safe, but I would do whatever it takes to keep them from harm. I owed it to her to at least try.

I launched myself into the air, sailing over the Calfkiller and towards the East. I paused midair, remembering someone else I hadn't said goodbye to. I turned and sailed over the trees and over the Deadwood. Full Spring had come and gone. When I touched down just outside the village, the normal hustle and bustle of a work day rose to my ears. Everyone had gone back to their daily lives.

I waited by the table where I had met Will last time. I saw him coming across the square and sent a gust of wind to direct him my way. He stumbled and looked up. He locked eyes with me and hurried across the weather-worn dirt paths, a small smile on his face.

He came and sat next to me. We both stared into the distance for a moment. "You look awful."

I took the chance to wipe the dirt on my pants and turn away from the rows of houses. "Thanks."

"Saxe left. I suppose that has something to do with it."

I nodded.

"You're leaving?"

"I have too."

He looked back towards his tiny village. "I understand." He looked back at me again. "Do you… want to talk about it?"

"I saw first hand why you call it Deadwood."

He tried to catch my eye. A single tear streaked down my face.

"I'm sorry. I hope you'll visit again. You're the only one who will play Bimsy with me. You made my life interesting for a little bit."

"Thanks, Will."

"I wish you well, Jack."

I smiled at him. "I wish you well."

I stumbled into the tree line with Lyla's staff leaning against my shoulders and my book under one arm. I flew over the trees and mountains. I followed the Calfkiller until my teeth chattered and I shook so badly I nearly fell out of the air. I crash landed in a tall pine overlooking a small village like Will's.

I slept on the rooftop of the nearest house, unwilling to speak to any of the locals or even steal some money. When I curled up next to the warmth of the chimney, I could see the stars peaking around the thin smoke. When I gazed into that vast abyss, I could almost imagine Saxe and Lyla sitting next to me. In the sunroom, Lyla would point out the "Gateway to the Gods" constellation every night. I'll never understand why she liked it so much. It was strangely silent without her by my side. I didn't trust myself to brave that silence.

"I miss you, Lyla," I whispered. The wind whisked away my words and hurled them into the darkness. "Keep her safe, old man." A falling star streaked across the darkness. I smiled and closed my eyes.

I reached the town Saxe had described just after nightfall the next day. I had picked up a cloak from an abandoned laundry line about an hour's walk from town. I had snatched a satchel before leaving the village I had stopped at to sleep earlier. The book thudded heavily against my leg as I walked into Town's Square. I pulled the hood tighter around my face and walked faster, hoping no one would notice me.

The fruit vendor had just finished closing up for the night. The rest of the stalls were boarded up and empty. The dark windows yawned at me like hollow shells of their former selves. I stopped dead in my tracks. I let my hood drop to see the full extent of my surroundings.

This was Carlin, arguably where the whole misadventure had started. I glared up at the sky. "Did you know the whole time?" I asked the darkness. "Is that why you let us get here before helping us?" As if in answer, clouds began to roll over the expanse of stars. I flew up to a thatched roof to oversee the city like a hooded vigilante. Carlin started to look more and more like when Lyla and I had been here only a few months prior. The fog settled in corners and on the roofs like snow. The clouds descended, and tendrils of fog began rolling down the streets like a giant snake.

I couldn't see the ground anymore. I took a deep breath and grasped Lyla's staff a little tighter. I jumped down, and the fog swallowed me whole. I wandered blindly through the thick fog. I could not cut through it with the staff's magic, and it seemed to corral me towards a back alleyway.

I came to a crossroads. At the center of the alley, a lamppost flickered dangerously close to extinguishing. The alley split into four different roads. One in front of me, one to the right, one to the left, and the one I came from.

For an instant, the mist cleared, and I saw three figures walking in my direction. Each came from a separate path, but we would all have to pass each other to continue our journey. I gripped Lyla's walking stick tighter.

This was it, the moment Saxe had been preparing me for. The moment he had died protecting.

We met in the fog.

# Acknowledgments

I began writing this series in April of 2020 when the Corona craziness was in full swing. I would sit through zoom calls and dream of a character who magically appears in the fog and dances through the cow fields in front of my house. I would jot down scenes in the margins of my composition books while doing history homework. While my English teacher talked about symbolism and themes in Hamlet, I'd take notes on how to add those thoughts into my own story.

Cole kept me company when the whole world was isolated and desperate. At night, I would imagine he was skipping down the barbed wire fence or beckoning me into an adventure from the halo of a streetlamp. I wrote the entire series in only three months. Without all the encouragement I received, Cole may have never existed anywhere beyond my imagination and a few notebooks.

I would love to give a huge thank you to my parents, who never stopped supporting me and my crazy dream. It was only by the grace of God that I made it this far. I am forever grateful for Mrs. Naaktgeboren. Without your honest encouragement and faithful editing, Cole may have never gotten to my readers. Thanks also to Mr. Crockett. Thank you for putting on a happy face when the whole world was falling apart and me teaching exactly what I needed to hear. I promise I was soaking up every word. A warm thank you to Mrs. Newton. Thank you for believing in me before I believed in myself. And to Mckena, who encouraged me through every draft. Thank you for being a prayer warrior.

One final word— to the dozens of agents, editors, artists, and publishing companies that turned me away— thanks for pushing me harder than anyone else ever could. I learned more from the pain of rejection and the sting of waiting than I ever would have if I had received a contract

offer the first time I queried. Sometimes waiting is not God

telling you no; sometimes, it is God telling you not yet.

# About the Author

Grace Edgewood is the author of the Fog Saga. When she is not cramming for exams, you can find her tucked away in a reading nook, with her nose buried in a children's novel. She was born and raised in the small town of Sparta, Tennessee, where she currently resides with her parents and younger sister. You can visit her at graceedgewood.com.

Photo taken by Olivia Merritt

Made in United States
North Haven, CT
06 May 2023

36318099R00219